Unexpected Love

A Novel by

Ka'Shus

KASHUS1NE PUBLICATIONS
BALTIMORE MD 21213
Kashus1nepublications@gmail.com

Printed in the United States of America

Publishers Note:
This book is a work of fiction. Names, characters, businesses, organizations, places, events and incidents are the product of the author's imagination or are used fictionally. Any resemblance of actual persons, living or dead, events, or locales is entirely coincidental.

For information regarding autographed copies or special discounts on bulk purchases, please contact Ka'Shus at *kashus1nepublications@gmail.com*

Library of Congress Catalog Card No.: On File

ISBN -10 0-9791876-3-X
ISBN-13 978-0-9791876-3-6

ACKNOWLEDGEMENTS

A special thanks first to the Lord above, for giving me the talent of imagination, and the writing skills. To my mother, love ones, brothers, friends, associates and even my enemies/non-believers:

I love you and thank you!

No names listed so there aren't any names missed.
I Love all of ya'll...

~Ka' Shus

Unexpected Love

Unexpected

When LOVE is planned upon
Two people
Bells may ring,
Doves may fly...
But when GOD given Love is anointed,
between two people...
it appears unexpectedly.
Bringing two souls
closer both willing to do
Anything for the other...
Many relationships end,
And many relationships last...
Which one is Yours?
Planned LOVE,
Or GOD given...
And if you still feel
You haven't found the one...
Stop planning, and prepare for the
UNEXPECTED...

Chapter one

Its night fall and Friday is finally here. Like every weekend routine, Kashmere, who is such the prettyboy standing at six-foot one, 200 lbs of pure muscle, light skin, bald is lying across a deep black couch calling and two-waying his brother-like friend Rodney. Rodney's another prettyboy who's six foot four, 215 lbs—also 100% muscle, bald but with a deep caramel complexion.

Every weekend it's the same thing, Rodney calls and says he's on his way but always runs late. Kashmere waits until midnight then he two-ways Rodney stating he'll meet him at the club. But on this particular night, while Kashmere's locking his door, Rodney's leaning on his midnight blue with gold trim Tahoe talking on the phone.

"Hold on…" Rodney says.

"What took you so long nigga!?" Kashmere yells out.

"Man, whateva, who's driving or are both of us doing our thing…?"

Kashmere starts unlocking his platium color E-Class Benz.

"Shit, you already unlocking your shit…you might as well follow me…"

"Where to? The usual spot or do you feel like going to DC, but I am tired of these bull-shit B'more clubs."

"Screw it den…hop in. I guess we going to DC…." Kashmere replies grabbing his Phatfarm leather which matches his outfit, then hops in the car. After locking up his truck, Rodney does the same thing, grabs his leather and leans back to enjoy the ride, returning back to his bullshit filled conversation.

Before hitting the Baltimore/Washington Parkway they stop by Crazy Johns carryout to grab a sub and some fries to prepare their insides for the liquor they were about to gulp as soon as they stepped foot in the club. After getting their order they went to the club. They were sitting at the bar of the famous 2 o'clock club watching the exotic dancers doing their thing.

"Yo, these dancers ain't shit compared to those DC shorties." Rodney points out as he orders a henne-coke.

"I feel you, but you know…" Kashmere starts to say before he's interrupted by the sight of this one dancer.

"What you say?"

"Nuttin, I didn't say shit."

"I'll be right back…." Kashmere responds while he approaches the dancer.

"How are you, Ms. Lady?" He questions as he sits beside her.

"I'm ok and you, cutie…?"

"I was doin' fine until she came onto me wit' that weak tip. Buy me a drink line…" he responds laughing. "Anyway, I'm Kashmere and you are?"

Just before she can open her mouth, the bartender interrupts asking if he wants to buy her a drink.

"Yeah, give her whateva she wants. I know she gots to make her money, but anyways, what your name again?" Kashmere repeats, paying for the drink and returning to the question at hand.

"Well my name is Sinsation…"

"Oh really, well I just wanted to get your name so if I come back I'll know who to ask for."

"Well, look, here's my card; give me a call. Do you have a pen so I can give you my home number also? 'Cause I'm not tryin' to lose you…" Sinsation responds writing her number down.

"We'll see what's up, don't let your man pick up the phone."

"I don't have no man…the only man I got is my son," Sinsation responds with an attitude.

"Calm down, ma, it's aiight. Yo, Rodney, let's be out." Kashmere hollers over to Rodney.

"Yeah, let's go 'cause this club is bullshit along with this bullshit drink," Rodney says walking toward the door.

"I'll holla at you, Ms. Sinsation," says Kashmere.

"Bye."

After leaving, they grab their food and continue to head for their planned destination.

"Shorty was all over you," Rodney mumbled while he took a huge bite out of his shrimp, cheese and steak sub.

"Naw, she was just doing her job, trying to make that dollar," Kashmere replies as he turns onto the Baltimore/Washington Parkway.

"OK, she could have been doing her job, but she still want your pretty ass…prettyboy…" said Rodney.

"Naw, I'm going to leave that prettyboy bullshit alone," Kashmere responds laughing.

"You pretty motha-fucka…"

"Whateva, you got me confused…damn this shit is good," Rodney continues demolishing his food.

A couple of hours pass and they find themselves at a personal VIP table with two of DC's finest dancers. The table is full of Henne and coke shot glasses. Rodney being drunk as much as usually tips both dancers around $300.00 a piece.

"Damn, that's how you feel, Rod?"

"Man, it's just money… I help the needy and I'm a need to put this money in those thongs," he replies lounging across one of the clubs couches.

Kashmere enjoying the show, but not really into it, suggests the dancers tag-up on Rodney who's stretched across the couch waitin' for a couple of lap dances. Hours fly by and they're both laid out on each couch. Kashmere calls girl to girl for Rodney's pleasure.

"Yo! Why are you just chillin' like that, let'n me get all this ass?" Rodney questions. "I'm not complaining, but Damn, good looking."

"No problem, son, get your fun all out 'cause they close in about thirty minutes anyway," Kashmere responds as he takes his drink to the head.

"Trust me, I am, cuzin! Trust me, I am."

During the let out of the club Rodney is leaning against the car talking to a dancer who calls herself Dream Xtcee. While Kashmere on the other hand, is laid back behind the wheel listening to a slow jam mix CD. He allows Rodney to finish his little QT 'macking then he rolls down the window and starts to interfere.

"Excuse me, can ya'll exchange numbers or better yet, hey, sweet heart, you can take his ass back to Baltimore. If you like…" he says with a smile on his face as Rodney looks at her.

"Oh I can do that, I live in Baltimore so that's no problem, but if I take him back he's not going home," she replies biting her bottom lip.

"Oh really? Yo, cuzin, I'll holla at you when I get back in town. Be safe," Rodney quickly responds grabbing his things out of the car then following Xtcee to her 2001 C-Class Benz.

"Damn! Shorty must got a good ass job other than dancing," Kashmere says to himself as he pulls off, heading for Baltimore.

The next afternoon, after Kashmere's hard day at work, he finds a message from Rodney on his cell marked urgent, telling him to call.

"Wzup cuzin? Everything aiight?"

"Of course… Yo, that shorty Xtcee can dance, but shorty can't fuck. After twenty minutes of bullshit I got up," Rodney says, his voice filled with frustration. "That was a waste of my time."

Laughing his ass off at Rodney, Kashmere responds, "Cuzin…was it that bad?"

"Don't get me wrong, the head was ablaze but the cakes was garbage, but I'm in the mood to teach cuz shorty got doe. For real… Look, meet me at my crib 'round 10:00 cuz."

"I'm 'bout to grab something to eat then take my ass to sleep, I'm tired!" Kashmere yells out pulling up to Poyeye's on Moravia Rd.

"Aiight cuzin…one hunit…"

"One hunit." As Kashmere said, he ate his food, but before he laid down he called Sinsation to see where her head was. He didn't receive an answer just a machine. So he left his number. Then he kept his word and went straight to bed. Just an hour into his sleep the phone began to ring.

"Hello," he answers with a raspy, sleepy voice.

"Hey, Kashmere, are you sleep?" The sweet voice asks.

"Yeah, who dis?"

"Sinsation, I'll call you back later, ok."

"Naw, I'm aiight just hold on," he quickly responds as he runs to wash his face to fully wake himself.

"I'm back, so wzup?"

"Nuttin, I didn't think you were going to call."

"I told you I would," answers Kashmere.

"Most niggas say that, just like most females tell niggas that, but don't do it," she explains. "But let's forget about all that bullshit, wzup wit you tonight? …I'm trying to see you."

"What, you want me to come down the club?"

"Naw, I'm talking 'bout after I get off."

"It's whateva…just call me, take my cell number down…"

"OK, what is it?"

They continue their conversation for at least two straight hours. Talking from goals all the way to exotic fantasies.

"Look don't talk about all this sex shit, and den don't do shit when we're together."

"Trust me, I will do everything I said plus more," Sinsation replies.

"Oh, aiight, we'll see whenever we hook-up," Kashmere says jumping to his feet. "Look, I'm going to call you back, let me take my shower."

"Damn, can I come join you?" she asks in an anxious tone.

"If you think your ready for all that, come on."

After that was said, she grabs a pen and pad then writes down his address.

While Kashmere waits, he tries to clean around the house a little. Thirty minutes pass and Kashmere is found in the doorway while Sinsation walks in covered in a blue silk robe with a black bag filled with essential body products and clothes.

"Well, hello to you, too," Kashmere says while she walks by.

"Hello, so where's the shower."

"Upstairs, come on," he replies as he looks up and allows her to lead him upstairs. He watches the jiggle of her ass with her every motion. Before he steps into the shower he lays her bag across his bed. When he returns to the bathroom all he sees is an hourglass figure image through the curtains.

"Are you coming in or do I have to wash my own back?" she questions as the water runs down her smooth caramel complexion skin.

"Here I come; damn you anxious."

"I am, so come on in," she replies pulling back the curtain.

She's standing there with beautiful skin, no stretch marks or bruises. Nice round breasts, a slim waist, nice thighs and pretty toes, along with her short twisted corn-rolls makes her the stunning attraction that catches everyone's eye when she's around.

"Damn you look good, bring your sexy-ass in here boy!" She continues on reaching out to him.

"Oh, you trying to be sweet and gentle…ah that's cute," Kashmere says with a smirk of enjoyment. When he is fully in the shower she gently eases him under the water allowing the water to flow down from his bald head to his toes. As her fingertips glide down his muscular body, Kashmere just trembles. Kashmere pulls her close to him.

"Damn you feel good, look good, got a gentle touch, where you been the past couple of years of my life?" Sinsation says as she places her lips upon his chest.

"Here, keeping to myself."

"Well I'm going to keep you all to myself, you can count on that."

A few minutes past and the once gentle kisses suddenly turned into smooth, slow licks, from head to toe, and toe to head. They both continue on with their seductive motives. When she makes a stop down below, Kashmere lays back his head allowing the warm flowing water to run across his face as his fingertips slide and grip her back, feeling her tongue twirl around his manhood. Standing at full attention, he carefully but quickly changes the role of the game.

"I wasn't finish…" Sinsation screams out. "What are you doing?"

"Do me a favor," Kashmere whispers out as he places her hands up against the wall.

"What?"

"Shut-up and let me do my thing, you got all day and night to finish."

"Who you think…" she begins to say, but is suddenly silenced as Kashmere's tongue glides across her smooth shaved lips of pleasure. Feeling this she instantly raises her leg and places it on the rim of the tub. In and out with a suck and delicate nibble upon her universal place of satisfaction, Kashmere sends an electrical surge up her spine, causing her body to quiver.

A couple of minutes of determination soar by. Then Kashmere is found drying her from head to toe, not missing a single inch. Once their bodies are completely dry, he sweeps her up off her feet and heads toward the bedroom.

During the few stops to the bedroom, Sinsation continues to kiss parts of his body that are within her reach. Finally, softly, he places her on the bed. They both continue to explore the foundation of excitement found below. With a simple flip, full erection plunges deep inside walls glazed in moisture, causing moans to rise and headboards to knock with a little bit of sheet gripping.

"Damn…" she moans out wrapping her legs around his waist.

Without any hesitation Sinsation has Kashmere grounded while she's squatting up and down on her newfound rod. The bed squeaks, sheets become undone as she releases the sexual beast from within. Hours go by and they've done positions not known to man. Suddenly the inner forces break through leaving them both curled together fast asleep.

It's almost that time, so Rodney decides to call to see if Kashmere has decided on his plans for the night.

"Hello?" Kashmere answers in a worn out drained voice.

"Wzup cuzin, you still 'sleep?"

"Yo, I just fell asleep, that shorty Sinsation is here."

"Who…? Oh, never mind," Rodney starts to ask then the name starts to ring a bell. "Where she at?"

"Right here, 'sleep."

"Oh, aiight, cuzin. When you get that broad out your house hit me up."

"Aiight…One hunit."

"One hunit..." Rodney replies as he tries to find something to do, while Kashmere returns to his nice slumber.

When Sinsation awakes she finds herself alsone in Kashmere's king size bed and Kashmere wrapped in a towel in his closet doorway. Not saying a word she jumps up and heads for the shower. By the time she finishes her relaxing period in the shower, Kashmere is dressed and waiting on Rodney to arrive.

"You going out?" she asks laying her clothes on the ironing board.

"Yeah, me and Rodney...why what's up?"

"Oh nuttin, so when we hookin' up again?"

"You want to hook up wit me again? I was that good...?" he questions with a devilish smile on his face.

"Just put it like this: if you weren't going out I would love to go for round two and three. Matter a fact make sure you bring your ass to my house after you are finished doing your thing," Sinsation replies while looking him up and down biting her lip.

"Aiight, that's fine wit me," says Kashmere.

"Just checkin'..." says Sinsation.

As soon as Rodney pulls up, Sinsation pulls off and passes him. Rodney does a simple wave and nod and heads for the house.

"So, what's up, cuzin? What's poppin'?" Rodney greets his people.

"Ain't shit, just chillin'. So what you trying to do?" Kashmere responds grabbing his leather and heading for the door.

"Wherever we end up, we end up, right?"

"Aiight, let's go."

As usual, they head for the bar to grab some Henne and coke then call to the usual chill spot known as the 'block.' They end up chillin' down there for the rest of the night, just drinking and chillin' with the rest of the crew.

Ka'Shus

When the clock says three in the morning, Kashmere's knocking at Sinsation's door. She comes to the door in her usual nightwear a long T-shirt with nothing underneath.

"Oh I thought you changed your mind…" she says as she heads back to her bedroom.

"Nice place, I see you like black and silver," Kashmere says as he browses around her two-bedroom town home. It is filled with black art and mirrors from wall to wall.

After giving himself a tour, he finds Sinsation lying in her bed asleep. Not disturbing her, he lays beside her and drifts off to sleep also.

Later on that morning, Kashmere is awakened by soft lips traveling down his back.

"You don't waste any time, huh?" he asks as his body tenses.

"Look, I apologize for falling asleep. Just shut-up so I can do my thing, OK? Thank you," she says continuing to let her lips explore his body. When she strikes the center of his back, Kashmere turns over to get the games truly started. But before that can happen, a knock comes at the door.

"Go get your door…" says Kashmere.

"Forget that door, I'm busy…" she replies as she starts from his chest on down. "If they really want something they'll come back. Plus everybody knows to call before they come unless I tell them otherwise," she explains.

Ten minutes passes and the knocking continues. Getting frustrated, Sinsation hops up to answer her door. After five minutes she returns to the bedroom to try to heat up the moment.

"So, you straight or is your man mad since your under cover busy at work?" Kashmere asks as she climbs back on top of him.

"Didn't I tell you I don't have a man? That was my neighbor seeing if she had to watch my son while I go to work," she responds while she moves her fingers across his body lightly.

"Now can I finish or do you have any other questions?"

Before he can answer, her phone starts to ring. After a glance at the caller ID she grabs the phone.

During her conversation, Kashmere's cell begins to ring also. It is Rodney.

"What's up cuzin?" he answers.

"Yo meet me on the block…" Rodney says in a scared tone.

"Yo, you aiight?"

"Naw, meet me at the block in ten minutes, aiight?"

"Aiight…one hunit…" Kashmere says getting dressed and heading out the door, not saying a word to Sinsation. When she finishes her conversation she returns to an empty room. She jumps back on the phone to see what's going on.

"Hello?" she says with an attitude.

"Look, my bad. Sin, I got to see what's up wit my peoples, he sounded scared and worried," Kashmere explains as she sits there quiet.

"Hello?"

"Oh, look, be careful and can you please come back over or at least call?" she says sounding concerned.

"You got that, ma…one hunit."

"Bye, Mr. Prettyboy," she says knowing she's about to start something.

"OK, so you want to start shit now, huh?" Kashmere says.

"What you going to do about it?"

"Just wait until I get back, but I'm on the block so I'll call you back."

"Aiight…be careful," she responds as she hangs up the phone.

Chapter two

When Kashmere arrives he finds Rodney being jumped by two unknown men. So without a second thought, he jumps out and runs to help even things up. Not knowing a thing that's going on, Kashmere drives one of the men's heads into the ground and begins to stomp the life out of him. Meanwhile, Rodney finds a way to grab a brick and smash the other man's face in, leaving him motionless. After allowing Kashmere to stomp the boy unconscious, Rodney finally decides to grab him and vacate the scene.

"Come on cuzin!" Rodney yells as he heads for his truck.

"Meet me 'round Cockee's." he continues, referring to a bar on East North Avenue.

"I'm right behind you," Kashmere responds while he gets his last few blows in.

Arriving a few minutes after Rodney, Kashmere parks and finds Rodney inside his truck with the usual Henne and Coke drink.

"So what da Fuck was all that about?" He questions Rodney as he steps into the truck.

"Oh, remember them niggas that was beefing like a year ago about my little cousin screwing one of their girls?"

"Yeah, why? Don't tell me all this shit is over a bitch," Kashmere yells out while taking a sip of Henne.

"Well yes and no," Rodney begins to answer. "The niggas shot my cousin in his leg over a broad and I whooped his ass over my cousin. So basically I was fighting for family…"

"Oh aiight, so is he aiight or what?"

"He's straight," Rodney begins to say when suddenly his cell begins to ring.

During Rodney's conversation Kashmere lays back to continue the intake of liquor.

Only staying on the phone for a couple of minutes, Rodney disconnects the call and plans to meet up with Kashmere later on that night. Before he lets Kashmere leave the truck, he thanks him for the help.

"No problem cuzin… You just call me wheneva you finish handling your business; I need to go eat," Kashmere replies closing the door.

"Aiight….one hunit."

The thought of Sinsation worring about him skipped Kashmere's mind as he heads home. Right after a long shower and quick snack he falls asleep for a couple of hours. Three hours past and Kashmere is found on the phone listening to Rodney describe this new dancer he spotted going into Foxie Ladee's, another one of Baltimore's strip joints.

"Yo, shorty is phat ass shit, cuzin, and she a sexy red bone."

"For real, let me guess that's where your trying to go tonight?"

"Of course…so I'll be there the usual time."

"Aiight… I'm going to grab something else to eat and some more drinks."

"Aiight, good looking," Rodney says, hanging up the phone.

Instead of cooking, Kashmere decides to order a sub and fries from North Star carryout. While his food is being made he stops by Cockees and grabs the drinks. When he arrives at North Star he enters with the usual call.

"Hey, daughter!" he yells out to the owner. "My food ready?"

No one really knows her name so they just call her 'daughter' and she replies. The same thing goes for her mother, everyone calls her 'mom'.

"Yeah", she responds with a Korean accent, as she exchanges food for money.

"Thanx, daughter!" Kashmere shouts out as he walks out the door.

Back at his house, Kashmere quietly sits on the front steps and starts to devour his food. While he watches the everyday action that occurs on his block, Rodney pulls up with his order from daughter's also.

"Wzup cuzin… I see you hit-up daughter's, too," Kashmere says taking another bite of his sub.

"Of course, you know I got to have my shrimp cheese steak to mix wit my Henne…"

"Oh, aiight."

Right after they eat, they continue to lay back for a while to at least drink half of their liquor. Just before they're ready, Kashmere's phone begins to ring, with Sinsation's number popping up on the ID.

"What's up ma…?"

"What, you forgot about me or something?" She questions.

"Naw, I've just been chillin' and making sure my people were aiight."

"Are they OK? Matter of fact, are you OK? I was worried," she says with a concerned voice. "Are you going out?"

"Yeah, I was on my way out the door now."

"Oh, my bad, are you coming over after the club?"

"I can do that. I'll call you when I'm on my way."

"OK, don't forget… Bye…" she says hanging up.

After he hangs up, Kashmere finds Rodney laid back in his truck waiting for him.

"Come on, nigga," says Rodney.

"Man, I'm coming… Go 'head, I'm right behind you…" he responds jumping in his car and pulling off.

It takes them ten minutes to get downtown. When they arrive at Foxies, the doorman greets them with the usual "Wzup". As soon as they step foot in the door, the dancers (which Kashmere and Rodney both know) come and hug them. During Kashmere's hugging process, Rodney orders the drinks from the bartender.

When he receives his drink from Rodney, Kashmere heads toward the pool table found in the back of the club. The first hour seems normal until the dancer Rodney was waiting for steps onto the stage. When her music begins, she gets into a sexual movement. Everyone's eyes are on her, even the other dancers giving the lap dances stop what they are doing to look at her.

"Yo, there she go…yo, she phat as shit!" Rodney said not taking his eyes off of her, but still able to hold a conversation.

"Damn, she is phat!" Kashmere responds lounging across the leather love seat located by the pool table. After she finishes dancing, she makes her way around the floor to make her rounds. Not far from Rodney, she starts to dance in front of Kashmere.

"What's your name, momi?"

"Kissable Lips, or just Kiss for short," she responds dancing with short blonde hair, nice firm thighs and stomach. She had a pair of breasts and an ass on her that would make a gay nigga drool.

"So, Kiss, do you have a man? If not, can I get your number?" He questions biting his bottom lip.

"No, I don't have a man and yes, you can have my number," she reaches for his two-way. While she types in her number, Rodney gives Kashmere a look like he's mad as shit.

The whole night passes and Rodney is not his usual self, he just ignores the fact that Kashmere got Kiss's phone number. Rodney just pulls another dancer and heads to his house with her. Then Kashmere heads for Sinsation's.

When he arrives there he uses the key that she had left for him in a hidden place. So after he lays his things down, Kashmere heads for her bedroom. He finds her laid quietly in her silk sheets, baring the untouched, soft caramel smooth texture plantation of nudity. Causing him to stare in full excitement at the innocent looking, but freakish devil in disguise, she lies there as he whispers out her name.

"Hey Sin…Sinsation?"

She starts to toss and turn like she is in the middle of a good dream. Kashmere tries calling out for her a couple of times, until he gives up and starts to make his expedition toward the treasure at hand.

He creeps his way onto the bed, not waking her as he eases the sheets down to the foot of the bed. As soon as he has comfortably situated himself, Kashmere gently starts to lick her ankles, then her calves, and finally her inner thighs, leading to the island of unforgettable wetness. Acting as if she doesn't feel a thing, Sinsation slightly helps him out by opening her legs to ease his struggles.

Not noticing that she is awake, Kashmere continues on with his voyage of pleasure by licking within the columns, which hold the key to all orgasmic stimulation. Within seconds, her silent state is broken as soft moans burst into the air.

Forgetting she wants to play along, she quickly grasps his head. Then she grabs the sheets, showing that he was inching his way to knock at her peak. Noticing what he's accomplishing, Kashmere speeds up the process. A chain reaction of chills shoot up her spine, leaving her in a daze of confusion, while tears of joy roll down her face.

Trying to hold her peace, Sinsation's pride is finally broken and she screams out.

"I can't take no more, but damn, boy..." she is unable to catch her breath to even continue her emotional outburst.

Taking this into consideration, Kashmere changes up to a slower rhythm to settle all the commotion down. Continuing this for just a few more minutes, he decides to move his way up the totem pole to get the sexual indulgement started. Filled with anxiety to satisfy Kashmere, to expose her gratitude, Sinsation gains inner power from some unknown place, flipping him to his back.

"Damn, it's like that huh?"

She yells out while he makes himself comfortable.

"Yeah, but you got to shut up so I can try to do my job and satisfy you," she responds kissing his chest.

From his chest, Sinsation heads in the direction of the staff of manhood which holds the fulfillment flow which is yearning to be released. With a suction motion from head to sac, she enjoys the hardness of his shaft rubbing across the jaws of her outer thoughts. Treating Kashmere like he is a blow-pop, she goes in search of the bubble gum center.

First she lets her tongue play for a while then allows the caramel stiffness to lay calmly as if she is putting it to rest. With Kashmere acting identical to Sinsation, but not totally gripping the sheets, he grazes his fingertips up and down her back. Making her mind wander, urging for the sight of Kashmere squirming, she begins to roll her tongue around the pulsing erected muscle inside her mouth. In one motion she gulps the moisture found within, which is released unbearably without control.

Once the last drop is invisible to sight, Sinsation continues to do what she knows best and gets the hardness to reappear as she takes a squatting position on her prey of delight. Hours pass and positions change, from her in a headstand to her legs wrapped around his neck.

Orgasm after orgasm, the passionate encounter continues. After every stroke and every position, they are both found laid back watching *The Best Man* on DVD.

"See niggas!" Sinsation yells out.

"What? Where the hell did that come from?" Kashmere asks in a state of confusion.

"The movie… A nigga got a good woman at home and he's worried about fucking an old friend," She says. "Just like a nigga."

"So, that's how you feel about all niggas?" he asks. "So, I guess that's how you feel about me?" Kashmere continues to pause the movie.

"Naw, boo, 'cause I know you know better… I dare you to try to inch somewhere else. I will cut your shit off, and that's a promise!" she responds snatching the remote from him and unpausing the movie.

"Whateva, you know I run shit," he quickly replies laughing. "I'm not even going there, all I got to say is try me."

"Whateva, boy," she says cuddling back up under him, nice and snug.

The movie is finally over and Sinsation being the main person wanting to watch the movie is fast asleep. Kashmere is left wide awake with nothing to do. He relaxes for an additional ten minutes then decides to go to Crazy John's on Baltimore Street to grab a bite to eat. Knowing he is going to hear Sinsation's mouth, he writes her a little note, letting her know what's going on.

When he arrives at Crazy John's, since it is so late in the morning, he orders his food and it's ready right away. Any other time it would take twenty to thirty minutes for a sub. Instead of going straight back to Sinsation's he decides to eat at home. Not meaning to, when he finishes eating he usually falls fast asleep. Well that is what happens and the consequences await him. Sinsation wakes up and finds him gone.

Chapter three

Its a new day and Kashmere is awakened by a banging on the door. For a good five minutes he ignores it until the banging gets louder.

"Motherfuckers must be crazy banging on my door like that," he thinks to himself as he jumps up. Not asking who it is he swings the door open yelling.

"What? Hello, Sin, how are you doing…"

"I'm here to talk to you about your Savior Jesus Christ," the Jehovah Witness says.

"Oh, hell, no!" Kashmere shouts out as he slams the door.

Changing routes towards upstairs instead of the couch he heads to his bed and falls asleep there. Kashmere sets his alarm so he will only sleep a couple more hours.

Kashmere hurries to get dressed and heads for his mother's. Just before he arrives, he phones her to find out if she needes anything from the store before he gets there.

"No, Kash, I don't need anything."

"Is anyone with you?" she questions, trying to be nosey.

"OK, and naw, there's no one with me, but I'm on my way."

"How long are you staying, because in like an hour I'm going to the Raven's game."

"Woman, I'm on my way!" he responds laughing.

"Nigga, please," she adds, laughing also.

"Bye, ma."

"See you when you get here."

Soon as he arrives all the neighborhood kids dart toward him speaking and hugging all on him.

"What's up ya'll? Ya'll been good?"

"Yeah, your mother in the house!" they all yell out.

"I know, that's why I came over here."

"Bye, Kaz!" the children yell out as they all hug him once again and continue on playing.

As soon as he enters the house, he spots his mother watching TV in the living room. She's covered in Raven's attire.

"Hey, woman," he says giving her a hug.

"Hey boy," she says.

"What you got to eat? 'Cause I'm hungry…" he asks heading straight for the kitchen.

"I don't know; you can have whatever you can find, but I'm about to go. Michelle is outside… Bye!"

"Bye, ma!"

As a usual routine when he visits his mother, Kashmere finds something to eat and lounges around watching TV. Wishing he'd bought a ticket, he turns on the game with the surround sound system blasting, so he can hear every hit and call. Feeling a little lonely, he decides to see where Kiss's head is.

"Hello?" she answers.

"Hey, Ms. Lady…dis Kashmere 'cause I know you got mad niggas."

"Shut up, boy, you crazy… What's up with you?"

"Nuttin', lounging over my mother's house, I came to visit her ass and she left and went to the Raven's game."

"For real? That's messed up," Kiss responds laughing. "So, other than that, what are you doing today?"

"Nuttin' really, I got a feeling someone wants to see me."

"It don't matter, it's up to you," Kashmere says showing he is not pressed if she comes or not.

"You want me to come to your mother's or what?"

"It really doesn't matter, you let me know what's up."

"Aiight, look give me thirty minutes then call me back, if that's OK with you?" Kiss asked while at the same time she looks for something to wear.

"That's cool…I'll call you."

"Aiight, bye."

Not really pressed, Kashmere doesn't move and continues to watch the game. At least an hour and a half goes by and he still hasn't called Kiss back. Deep into the game Kashmere doesn't pay attention to how time has flown by. Before the game is about to end, the phone rings.

"Hello?"

"What happened to you calling me?" Kiss asks in a foul tone.

"Damn, I totally forgot, my bad. So do you still want to hook up or did you change your mind?"

"What's the address?"

Kashmere spends a couple of minutes telling her the directions to his Mom's. Afterwards, he continues to watch the game not really believing that she's on her way. Down to the final seconds of the game, there's a knock on the door.

"Who is it?" Kashmere yells out not looking out the peephole.

"It's Kiss. Open the door, boy."

"I didn't think you were coming," he says opening the door looking her up and down.

"Didn't I tell you I was coming, unlike you returning phone calls…" she says laughing giving him a hug.

"Thank you…so what's going on?"

"Nothing, working and chilling."

"So, you not working tonight?" Kashmere questions lying back across the coach.

"Yeah, but I figured I would stop by to say hello, and to see if you were as fine as you were in the club. 'Cause you know, clubs lights play tricks on you sometimes."

"So, did they play tricks on you or what?"

"Hell, not… I love what I see!" she says sitting across the room on the love seat.

"OK, we'll see how long this attraction will last," Kashmere responds sarcastically.

"I guess I got to prove it to you."

"If you want."

Hours pass and they learn each other's satisfying qualities dealing with their mental and emotional standards. It seems like they tell each other their life stories.

After their long conversation, they both leave his mother's house and head on their separate ways. Kashmere goes home and Kiss goes downtown to work. On his way home, Kashmere calls his friend Dayshanae to check if she is home so he can see her.

After he confirms she is home, he goes to lay back with her and chills for the remainder of the day. Everytime Kashmere and Dayshanae got together they both explained that they don't think of themselves like that, only friends.

When he arrives at her house Dayshanae is on the porch along with her grandmother enjoying the weather, while the baby pitbull plays in the yard. Not knowing him very well, when Kashmere enters the gate, the dog goes crazy and starts barking.

"Menace! Menace, calm down boy!" Dayshanae yells out as the dog calms down and begins to sniff Kashmere.

"You better get this crazy dog before I kick it."

"You better not kick my dog, boy," Dayshanae responds as she hugs him.

"There go, grandma."

"Aww, shit, here we go," he whispers in her ear. "Hey, grandma, how you doing?"

"I'm OK, baby… I know you couldn't stay away for long," she says covered in a knitted blanket with her hair wrapped up like she was 'Aunta Mama'.

"Let's go in the house before she gets started," Dayshanae says pulling him into the house, straight to her room. Lying across her bed, Dayshanae looks sexier than ever. She's about five foot one, weighing 135 lbs, pretty gray eyes and long reddish brown hair.

"Damn, your room ain't changed a bit," Kashmere says lying back in her computer chair.

"Was it supposed to? You didn't change either…you got a little cuter though," she responds smiling, putting her head back into her pillow.

"Oh really, so how you think I'm cute?"

"I always thought you were cute, I just didn't say anything," she says sitting up and looking him in the eyes. As they both inch closer to each other they can only say one word.

"Really?" Kashmere whispers.

"Yeah."

Just when their lips start to touch, Kashmere's phone begins to ring. "Damn, hello?" he answers the phone, leaving Dayshanae frozen in amazement.

She gets up and goes to check on her grandmother. When she returns, Kashmere is looking at an old picture of him and Dayshanae. A smile appears across his face.

"What's up with that smile?" she asks, lying across her bed.

"Oh nothing, we just look so cute back in those days, like we were in love or something."

"Well I…." she begins to say.

Kashmere whips his head around. "Naw… What were you going to say?"

"Nothing."

"That's bull-shit… You know I hate it when you start something and don't finish."

"Are you talking about how you just left me a minute ago?" Dayshanae said turning her head.

"What are you talking about? I mean, you lost me... for real."

"So you weren't ready to kiss me just a minute ago? Or was I just imaging that...?" She responds looking him in the eyes.

"Yeah, but..."

"But what, Kashmere?"

"We can't do that, it will mess up our friendship."

"Naw, I don't think it would, we would just be expressing our true feelings."

"You cool and everything, you'll always be cool in my book... because you my best friend," Kashmere says walking towards the door.

"Look I'm gonna see what's up with my peoples and I'll be back... No disrespect to you, I'm just not trying to mess up our friendship."

"Kashmere, wait!" Dayshanae shouts out jumping to her feet. "I got to tell you something," she continues as her eyes begin to water.

"What...What's wrong, shorty?"

"You said you didn't want to mess up our friendship and I hope this doesn't fuck it up but..." she pauses.

"What...? There you go doing that bullshit again," he says leaning against the wall. "What's up?"

"Kashmere."

"Yes, Dayshanae?" he responds with a smile.

"Kashmere I love you, and I fell in love with you the first time we ran into each other in the hallway in Chinquapin Middle. Look I love you and I want you."

"Girl, stop playing with me," Kashmere says laughing until he spots that Dayshanae isn't laughing. "Damn, you serious, aren't you?"

"Just forget it."

"Naw look, I'm sorry," he says grabbing her hand, stopping her from walking away. "Look I didn't know you were serious, we always be playing."

"No, you always are playing, and I am serious."

"Well I didn't know."

"Now you know… your best friend fell in love with you…" Dayshanae responds.

"I hope you don't leave me alone like you did a minute ago," she continues inching in for a kiss. Not pulling away from the kiss, deep into the moment, Kashmere says something that shocks Dayshanae.

"I love you, too, but I need to think… I'm sorry," he says as he walks down the stairs and out the door.

Chapter four

With all emotions in the air Kashmere tries to keep his distance from Dayshanae, trying not to cause feelings to grow anymore than they have. Two weeks pass and they haven't talked, not even once. Until one day, while Kashmere is pulling up to his house he spots Dayshanae lounging on his front steps.

"What's up, Day…? What you doing here?"

"What, I open my heart to you then you cut me loose?" she asks sitting on the steps with her hands crossed in between her legs.

"Naw, it ain't like that. Like I told you before, I'm not trying to mess up our friendship. Trust me it would mess it all up to the point that we wouldn't even look each other's way," he says sitting down beside her.

"How you figure, Kashmere?"

"'Cause friends and relationships never work."

"But if you want it to work, it can work itself out and I think it will work."

"No it wouldn't, 'cause for one, you know I got a shorty and two, you are my best friend. That would really mess it up," Kashmere says trying to explain to her in a straight up way not holding nothing back, but also trying not to hurt her feelings at the same time.

"I know all about her but ya'll not together or comitted are ya'll?"

"You might as well say we are 'cause if you see me, you'll see her."

"OK we use to be like that," she starts to say before she's cut off by the ringing of Kashmere's phone.

"Hold that thought," he says to her as he answers his phone. "Hello?"

"Hey, boy, where you at?" Sinsation questions him.

"Sitting on my steps talking to one of my best friends I grew up with."

"Who?"

"My homegirl, Dayshanae. Why, what's up?" Kashmere says.

"Nothing, call me when she leaves," Sinsation responds as she suddenly hangs up the phone without saying goodbye.

Noticing she hung up so abruptly, Kashmere looks at the phone in shock.

"What's wrong?" Dayshanae asks, being the concerned friend she's always been.

"Yo, she hung up on me!" he says, still in shock.

"Why? 'Cause you told her I was here?"

"I don't know, but I'm going to find out," Kashmere says as he redials Sinsation's number.

"What!" She answers after looking at the caller ID before picking up the phone.

"What is wrong with you?" Kashmere questions with frustation in his voice.

"You pushing me to the back burner for that bitch?"

"What? You the one that hung up on me when I told you she was here…she knows all about you and she's just a friend anyhow. She has been by my side since middle school."

"Whateva, Kashmere… I'll call you back," Sinsation responds after listening to Kashmere plead his side of the story.

"What?" Kashmere responds once again listening to dead air. Allowing Sinsation to cool off, Kashmere returns to his conversation with Dayshanae.

"So, she hung up 'cause you told her I was here right? And don't lie."

"Yeah, but I don't know why... She never acted like this before."

"Look, I'm not trying to come between ya'll so call me later... But if you didn't know already, I'll always be here for you," Dayshanae replies as she kisses his cheek and walks off towards her car.

"So, you leaving?"

"Yeah, I'll call you when I get home."

"Aiight," Kashmere responds as she takes off down the street.

Calm and settled back in the house, Kashmere lays across the couch while he checks out what's coming on TV. Deciding not to call Sinsation right back, he leaves the TV on the menu and goes to grab a bite to eat out of the kitchen. Just before he reaches the kitchen, his cell phone begins to ring showing Sinsation's number across the screen.

"Call my house," Kashmere answers.

"OK," she responds hanging up. Seconds later his phone starts to ring.

"What's your problem, yo?" Kashmere questions, not even saying hello.

"What are you talking about?" She responds playing stupid.

"You know...all the bitch calling and hanging up."

"Look, I apologize OK? I had some shit on my mind and you were the only one around," she responds in her most sincere voice.

"Man, don't give me that sexy voice bullshit...you know you were wrong that's why you're changing your voice," Kashmere responds. "Look, let me grab something to eat and I'll call you back."

Just before he can open the cabinet there is a knock on the door interrupting his food gathering.

"Who is it?" he questions as the person knocks again. "Who *is* it?" he asks again. "Oh, what's up, I thought you were going home?"

"I was, but I wanted to finish talking…that's if it's alright with you?"

"Look come on in 'cause you are messing up my eating process," he responds turning around and heading for the kitchen.

"Look, nigga, sit your ass down. I'll cook you something to eat," Dayshanae says tugging at his pants and pulling him out the way.

"Shit, you ain't got to tell me twice," he responds heading straight for the couch.

Five minutes into her cooking, there is a knock at the door. Not budging, Kashmere looks at Dayshanae like she's crazy trying to answer his door.

"Who is it?" he yells out opening the door to notice Sinsation standing there trying to look sexy.

"Hey you," she says pushing him out of the way and walking into the house. Once her foot hits inside the house, she spots Dayshanae in the kitchen. Everything becomes quiet as Dayshanae and Sinsation look at each other in shock.

"Oh, hell no!" Sinsation yells out dropping her pocket book on the floor.

"Yo, it's not like…" Kashmere starts to say when Sinsation cuts him off.

"Shut up!" she yells out as she walks towards Dayshanae.

"Hey, girl!" Sinsation says as they hug.

"What?" Kashmere yells out.

"Boy, calm down. This is my girl from way back," Sinsation says. "If I would have known it was her…" she begins to say, but instantly stops. "Oh my goodness, it just hit me. This is the nigga you always talking about when we are on the phone isn't it?"

"Yeah, girl, but I see you got him," Dayshanae responds returning to her cooking.

"Girl, I'm so sorry. You never told me his name. I'm so sorry," Sinsation says as a tear rolls down her face, noticing the hurt in Dayshanae's face.

"Look, I'm sorry Dayshanae. I didn't know how you felt in the beginning and I didn't know you knew her," Kashmere says with a concerned look on his face.

"It's aiight…you didn't know," Dayshanae says.

He turns around and heads toward the couch.

During their time alone in the kitchen, the girls engage in a deep conversation about Kashmere. As they conversate, Kashmere relaxes across the couch and falls asleep. An hour passes and he wakes up to find them eating dinner together quiet as hell.

"Look, I feel real bad about me and you, now that I know my girl's in love with you. I just have feelings for you, but she is in love with you, so ya'll need to work that out," Sinsation explains to Kashmere.

"I feel you, but me and her are too good of friends. A relationship would mess that up."

"Not if you don't allow it to. Look I'll call you later. Ya'll need to talk," Sinsation says getting up and placing her plate in the sink. Then she walks out the door.

With her being gone, Dayshanae and Kashmere still sit in silence as they finish their dinner. Not saying a word to each other, Dayshanae finally finishes her dinner, washes her plate and walks straight out the door leaving Kashmere alone at the table. When she gets halfway down the block, she calls Kashmere.

"Hello?" he answers.

"Look, I'm sorry for walking out, but I figured it out. We wouldn't work out 'cause if we did hook up then if we broke up I wouldn't know how to act around you."

"It's hitting you now, but when I said it before you got mad…but I understand now. Let me wash these dishes and I'll hit you back," he responds as they hang up the phone.

While he washes up the dishes all he can think about is the whole situation of them knowing each other. *Damn, what the hell am I going to do now?* he thinks to himself.

Chapter five

The next day Kashmere is found on the phone with Dayshanae for two hours while at the same time eating a quick meal from McDonalds.

When the third hour rolls around there's suddenly a knock at the door. The second he opens the door, Sinsation starts to rub his six pack stomach.

"Hey baby…forget what I said yesterday I can't let you go," she says not knowing Dayshanae can hear her every word.

"Yo, chill, I'm on the phone with…" he starts to say but is cut off by Sinsation.

"And just to think I was going to let you go for her. I know we cool but fuck that, I'm not letting you go unless you tell me to get lost. What was I thinking about…for real? Fuck, Dayshanae."

"Sinsation, yo, if that's your girl you need to chill 'cause she's on the phone," he responds not knowing that Dayshanae had hung up after hearing the words 'Fuck Dayshanae.'

"Hello….Hello?" he repeats.

"See, that bitch don't care, she's hanging up and shit," Sinsation says continuing to rub on his stomach, heading towards his muscular rod, trying her best to get started on their usual encounters.

"There's someone knocking on the door," Sinsation says. "Now who the hell is that?" Sinsation yells out heading towards the door. She hadn't locked the door before they got started. Dayshanae busts straight through the door connecting her fist to Sinsation's right jaw.

"Fuck 'who' now, bitch?" Dayshanae shouts as she continues to connect blows from Sinsation's head to her kidneys.

In between one of Dayshanae's forceful connections, Sinsation gracefully finds a way to reach out and push Dayshanae's temple, knocking her to the ground. They are wrestling across the floor when Kashmere tries to break them up. Through all the commotion, Kashmere and Dayshanae don't notice Sinsation pull out a box cutter. She takes three good swipes, not caring who she hits, then gets up and runs out the door.

As she runs out, she leaves behind a bloody trail. Kashmere has two gashes in his arm and Dayshanae has one in her thigh. Luckily Rodney pulls up as Sinsation races down the street. Not paying her any attention, he walks in the house like he usually does.

"Yo, what the hell you do to that girl…'cause…" he starts to say when he finally spots the situation.

"Oh shit!" he yells out as he grabs the phone to call for help.

Not surprised by the long wait for help, Rodney decides to take them to the emergency himself. Within hours, everybody is back at Kashmere's talking about the whole thing, leaving Rodney in tears from all the laughter.

"Yo, it ain't that funny, but you should of seen ya'll faces when the doctor was stitching ya'll up."

"Man, forget you," Kashmere starts to say before he is interrupted by a knock on the door.

"Who is it?" Rodney shouts out as he opens the door to find EMTs with the police.

"Did ya'll dial 911?"

"Yeah, like hours ago, everything is aiight now."

"Well sir, if you could have taken care of it yourself you shouldn't have called us," one of the officers suggests.

"Whateva, man. Fuck that, ya'll took so long that I handled shit myself... But thanks anyway," he responds as he closes the door.

Before he can leave the door, the same officer knocks again. Twenty minutes of arguing goes from Rodney getting a warning for disrespecting an officer to him getting locked up for putting his hands on an officer.

Kashmere quickly hops up to try to see if he can settle the problem, but it's worthless as the officer turns around to show his busted lip.

Still in pain, Kashmere and Dayshanae head for central booking to get Rodney released. During his booking, Rodney can not shut his mouth and makes matters worse. Being the friends they are, Kashmere along with Dayshanae explains what happened over and over again trying to get him released.

"If your boy doesn't shut up, he's going to be in here more than he has to be, just for running his mouth," the officer says as he looks up Rodney's bail.

"Yo, Rodney, shut up!" Kashmere yells as Rodney continues to run off at the mouth.

"Look, I'm going to give you one more chance to calm your boy down, or his ass is going in the back," the officer says.

"Yo, Rodney, just shut up so we can get the hell out of here."

Noticing how serious Kashmere is, Rodney decides to bite his lip, so he can go home.

After four hours of paperwork, attitudes and money exchanging; Rodney is finally released.

Back at Kashmere's, Dayshanae lays calmly across the bed fast asleep while Kashmere and Rodney recap again what happened from the fight to Rodney getting locked up.

"Yo, that shit was funny," Rodney says while he starts to laugh.

"What?"

"How I was pissing those cops off… Did you see how red those white ones were?"

"Man, they were going to throw you dumb ass in jail," Kashmere responds laughing.

"I could have stopped before it got to that point. That's why I stopped when I did."

"Whateva you say, nigga," Kashmere mumbles as he searches through his DVD movie collection.

"Yo, what you got to eat?" Rodney questions as he heads for the kitchen. Being the lazy person he is, Rodney notices that everything he wants to eat has to be cooked so he decides to order out.

"Yo, since your bitch ass is hurt and I feel sorry, I'll pay for the food," he explains to Kashmere laughing.

"Yeah, aiight as long as you order enough for all three of us."

"Nigga, I know."

Dinner arrived a couple of minutes later, and Kashmere sees if Dayshanae is ready to eat. Still in pain, she decides to eat later. While they eat their food, Rodney brings up a question that he just happens to think of.

"Yo, did you sleep with Dayshanae yet?"

"Naw, we friends."

"So let me get this straight, you got stabbed up over some cakes you didn't even get?" He responds with a mouth full of food.

"Damn, that kiss must have been off the hook," he continues laughing.

"It's not even like that, I mean I care for her but I've always looked at her as my friend."

"I feel you on what you saying, and I know she feels the same way, but just a little more. If it came down to it both of ya'll wouldn't stop. I know I never said nothing about relationships but I think she might be the one, for real, but that's my opinion," Rodney expresses his feelings as he continues to stuff his face.

"Anyways, yo, I'm 'bout to go 'cause I can't be like you without no cakes." He adds laughing as he finishes his food and walks out the door.

"Aiight yo, just holla at me tomorrow."

"Oh and think about what I just said." Rodney suggests while he pulls off, leaving Kashmere deep in thought.

Ka'Shus

Chapter six

Taking Rodney's opinion deep into consideration, Kashmere decides after a couple of days of healing he wants to sit and try to express his feelings toward Dayshanae. He hopes she will understand and express her feelings, too.

Throughout the whole conversation he explains that he sees her as a good friend and no more. But on the other hand, Dayshanae explains her feelings in another way. In tears, crying out that she has strong feelings towards him and he's all she wants.

"Look, no disrespect to you, but like I said before, that will mess up our friendship. I'm not going to lie, I got mad love for you, but I'm not ready for us to hook up," Kashmere says.

"You always talking that bullshit. If you want me what's the fucking problem? I understand about messing up the friendship, but it will work out if we really want it."

"That may be true, but I'm not trying to take that chance right now…OK?" he explains.

"OK, whateva, so I got in a fight over your ass, got stabbed and I still can't have you… That's bullshit, man, for real. Maybe you and that crazy bitch should stay together," she says as she storms out the door.

"Dayshanae…Dayshanae?!" Kashmere screams out as she pulls off.

For the next ten minutes, he tries to call Dayshanae, but ends up unlucky. Everytime he calls she picks up then instantly hangs up. Without making himself look like a fool, Kashmere finally decides to give up and give her time to cool off. For the rest of the day he lounges around watching movies and sleeping.

The next day Kashmere is awakened by Rodney, banging on the front door.

"Get up nigga!" Rodney yells out.

"What's up, yo?" Kashmere replies in a sleepy worn out voice.

"You feel like going to ball?" Rodney asks as he starts to dribble the ball.

"It's whateva, give me bout ten minutes."

"Aiight, go 'head I'll just raid your fridge like always," Rodney says laughing.

Twenty minutes passes and they're on the blacktop looking for teammates. During their search, Kashmere notices Sinsation looking through the gate, looking at the other game. Thinking about the drama she put him through, he ignores her and focuses on the upcoming game. Fifteen minutes into the game, Kashmere's team is up by twenty points and everything he makes, a move or a dunk, all he hears is Sinsation yelling out his name. After the game she decides to approach him.

"Hey Kashmere."

"What's up?" he responds, not really paying her any mind.

"Look, I apologize for that bullshit situation the other night, it shouldn't have happened. You weren't suppose to get hit."

"OK, whateva, but I did so let's leave it alone."

"Leave what alone?" she asks.

"This conversation," he responds as he walks away toward his car.

"So, it's like that? I apologized."

"OK, and that apology doesn't take the damn scars away!" he shouts out as he races off down the street with Rodney not too far behind.

Back at home, Kasmere notices that he has a message on the phone. After listening to Dayshanae apologize and also fuss, he heads upstairs to take a long shower. Following his shower he tries to get dressed but is interrupted by the sound of knocking on the door. Still wrapped in a towel he races down the stairs.

"Who is it?" he yells out.

"Sinsation."

"Who?"

"Now you playing, can you please open the door?" she starts to beg, as he opens the door.

"What's up, ma?"

"Damn, you look good, can I take that off?" She questions as she bites on her bottom lip.

"Naw, I might get stabbed," he responds laughing. "But are you coming in or not?" he continues while she strolls inside.

"So, what? I can't get no hug now?" She asks.

"For what, and why are you here?" He grabs a pair of shorts that are lying around.

"Damn, I came by to talk about what happened and to see if I could have a chance back with you."

"Whateva…why should I take you back? Give me one good reason!" he yells out.

As he tries to begin another statement, she pulls him close and begins to kiss him, interrupting any idea or conclusion that comes into his mind.

"Yo, what are you doing?" he questions as he pushes her away.

In the process of pushing her away, she takes her hand and gently grabs his rod of manhood. Allowing temptation to take it's course his shorts fall, his shirt and jeans disappear as bodies became one.

Like the world always says, make-up sex is always the best sex. Starting on the couch, tongues were reintroduced to body parts not thought of by man.

Sinsation, being the undercover freak she is, had Kashmere stand up against the door as she began to do her thing. Standing on her hands she starts to lick the part he adores so much. Round and round her head moves while he struggles to hold his pride inside. As his pole knocks on the back of her throat he suddenly lets go, leaving her bent over backwards with her not missing a stroke.

Ten minutes fly by and she's still in the same position with no complaints. As she takes a breather, he grabs her back, bends over and begins to lick the tiny key that opens the gates to uncontrollable body quivers with unstoppable flows of wetness. With her bridge breaking down, they head for the couch where he takes a plunging dive inside the walls of everlasting bliss. Getting tired of trying to get comfortable, they decide to relocate to the bedroom while hours pass and sweat begins to pour as they explore horizons of each other until they both drop from exhaustion.

"Damn nigga, we need to fight more often," Sinsation suggests as she lets out a soft exhale.

"Whateva…" he responds by laughing, "so now you want to be back with me, huh?"

"You think I'm giving that up…you must be crazy?" she says as she gathers her clothes and heads for the door.

"I'll call you when I get home."

"Aiight, you might have to call my cell 'cause I might not be here," he says.

"OK!" she hollers back as she walks out the door.

When she's out of sight, he runs upstairs to hop in the shower once again. But this time when he's finished he receives a call from Rodney telling him to meet up with him.

Rushing to get dressed he runs out and meets Rodney at the Security Square Mall where Rodney is posted against his truck. "What took you so long? Rodney asks.

"I had some unexpected company from Sinsation," he responds with a sly grin on his face.

"Aiight, you keep messin' with that crazy-ass girl if you want to," Rodney warns. "Don't say nothing when she cuts your ass again."

"Shut up, nigga, so what's up?" Kashmere asks as he gets out of the car.

"Yo, I'm trying to get out of Baltimore. You got any ideas."

"This shorty I know wanted me to come visit her down in Georgia."

"For real, what she do down there?"

"She goes to Spellman, and she got mad friends," Kashmere said with a big grin on his face.

"When you trying to go?" Rodney asks filled with excitement.

"I'll let you know tonight, I got to call her and see when she is free."

"Aiight, that's cool… I'm about to go get something to eat if you are trying to roll," Rodney says while he jumps up in the truck and decides what CD to listen to.

"I'll be right behind you."

After close to forty-five minutes of driving they arrived at Dave and Busters in D.C. While they wait to be seated, nothing but sexy groups of females enter in and out the door. While her friends are adding their names to the waiting list one girl sits down and asks Rodney who's with him.

"My boy, right, that's it…matter a fact, hey Ms. Lady, you can put them with us," he suggests. "That's if it's aiight with you, Kashmere, and you, Ms. Lady?" Rodney asks the girl and her friends.

"It's cool," Kashmere replies.

"Yeah, you can put us together," her friend whispers with a smirk on her face. As she says that, the other host comes to say that their table is available. When he notices that two more people have been added to the list he quickly switches them to a booth. While they get settled and introduced to their waiter, Kashmere remembers that he doesn't know these females' names.

"Oh yeah, my name is Kashmere and you are?"

"Oh, damn, my bad I'm Stacey, nice to meet you," she responds as they shake hands.

"You not going to ask my name?" her friend asks.

"I ain't worried about it, you wit my boy," he says laughing. "Naw, what's your name?"

"Forget you, Kashmere…my name is Danna and you are?" turning her head to Rodney ignoring Kashmere with a smile on her face.

"I'm Rodney."

"OK since that's out the way. I need to let you know, Stacy, I'm broke so you got to pay," Kashmere says laughing.

"OK, that's no problem."

"Oh shit, I was just playing, but if you don't mind," he says grabbing the menu. Let me get you the most expensive thing," he laughs.

"I was playing, too, you better get ready to wash dishes," she says laughing.

"Oh aiight, let me move then," he says acting like he's moving.

"Boy, you better sit yourself down."

During their time of joking Rodney and Danna sat cuddled up looking into a menu like they were friends forever.

"Look at this I'm about to be sick…. All this lovey-dovey stuff," Kashmere says making a sick sound.

"Me, too. Call the waiter, I think they need their own table," Stacy says laughing.

"Bye…and he can take you home, too," Danna says laughing.

"I sure can as long as she's got gas money," Kashmere responds laughing.

"Oh, for real," Stacy says laughing as her and Kashmere began to play fight. They all began to laugh.

They end up at Danna's after their two hours of eating and joking at Dave and Busters. Not staying long, they exchange numbers and Kashmere and Rodney head back to Baltimore.

Back at Kashmere's, Rodney reminds Kashmere to talk to his friend in Georgia, then heads home. Once he's laid up across his bed watching a movie called *Belly*, he gives her a call. After about three rings a sweet, exotic voice picks up.

"Hello?"

"What's up ma?"

"I'm aiight, boy, what's up with you?" she replies.

"Ain't nothing…. Hey Shavon, what you doing in a couple of weeks, 'cause me and my peoples trying to come down."

"For real? Don't bullshit wit me. My roommate can chill wit your boy," she says filled with excitement.

"Aiight, tell her his name is Rodney. Hold up, how she look?"

"Remember the light skin girl that was in the picture with me that I sent you?"

"Yeah…she cute and phat."

"See, I'm going to ignore that…but that's her."

"Oh aiight, that's cool… Look find out what days is cool for ya'll and let me know!" he says.

"Aiight, hold on I just got to check my track schedule."

"How 'bout her?" He questions.

"She run track wit me and she sitting right her with a big smile on her face, 'cause she looking too damn hard," she says laughing. "But we free the first week of December, is that cool?"

"Yeah, look, I'm going to call Rodney," he begins to say before Shavon cuts him off.

"Rodney… ain't that the nigga that look like your twin?"

"Yeah, why?" he questions.

"I was asking 'cause she was wondering how he looks, but what were you saying?"

"I'm going to call him and then we going to get the plane tickets and let you know what time to come get us, OK?"

"OK, Kashmere, don't have me waiting and you bullshitting."

"I'm not, you'll know by tonight I promise."

"OK, bye."

"Bye, girl."

As soon as he hangs up he runs to his computer to check some prices and to call Rodney. After looking up the prices and hearing Rodney's reaction they decide to leave on the first and return on the early morning of the fourth. Keeping his promise, he returns his call to Shavon.

"Hey ma."

"So what's up?"

"Look we leaving on the first and coming back on the fourth… So I'll be there 'round noon aiight?" he explains to her.

"Aiight, I wrote it down so I'll see you," Shavon responds.

"Aiight," he responds as they both hang up the phone.

The following day, Kashmere and Rodney go out and purchase new sneakers along with outfits.

"Yo, it's going to be off the hook," Rodney says.

"Yeah, I know" Kashmere responds as they finish their shopping, then head home.

Chapter seven

The day has finally come and they are pulling into Hartsfield Atlanta International Airport at noon, on time. On their way up the ramp, they spot Shavon with her friend before anyone. They both have white and red Spellman half tees with a pair of shorts that even a blind person could see their kitty prints. On her first sight of Kashmere, Shavon sprints and leaps into his arms. After a long ten minutes of lustful hugs, she finally introduces her friend to both Kashmere and Rodney.

"Excuse me, my bad…" Shavon starts to say before she's interrupted.

"Forget you… Hi Kashmere, hi Rodney, I'm Dejah," she announces with a tasteful smile. Both stand at five eight and 152 lbs apiece. Muscular calves, strong thick thighs, with flat stomachs, which bring them to the center of attention. Shavon has light green eyes with matching, enticing lipstick that helps take the attention off her firm breasts and yellow-tinted skin.

Now Dejah, on the other hand, has light hazel eyes, mild caramel skin and a body that's a head turner—enough to cause both Kashmere and Rodney to slip into a daze.

"Ya'll better come on, ya'll only here for a couple of days," Shavon reminds them.

"Shit, screw that. We can go to a hotel. I'm not trying to go back until next weekend. I got to see more of Spellman along with Georgia that a weekend can offer," Rodney says as he casually hangs his arm around Dejah's neck.

"I'm feeling that," Dejah replied.

"Yo, it's whateva," Kashmere agrees in his own original way.

"Aiight, so ya'll need to change ya'll's ticket dates," Shavon suggested. "Then we can get ya'll's rooms reserved."

Taking her advice, they quickly grab their luggage and change the dates. On their way to Spellman, Rodney's phone begins to ring.

"Hello?"

"Hey sexy... this is Danna."

"Hey, ma, look I'm in Atlanta right now so I'll hit you up when I get back to B'more."

"Aiight….bye."

"Aiight," he replies. Instead of hanging up he simply turns off the phone.

"You might as well put that phone up, too, Kashmere. 'Cause ya'll about to forget all about Baltimore, 'cause we about to turn ya'll out," Dejah yells out.

Dejah smiles at Kashmere. "Well I don't know about you, Kashmere, but I guarantee Rodney's going to be climbing the walls…matter a fact, when we get to the school me and you going to get that room ASAP!"

"Damn, it's like that, but I doubt that turning out bullshit," Rodney talks shit as usual.

"OK, we'll see."

"We sure will," he replies smiling.

Kashmere and Shavon just sit quietly gazing into each other's eyes every moment they get. The minute they arrive at Spellman, Rodney and Dejah are nowhere in sight. Ignoring the fact that they are gone, Kashmere and Shavon head to her dorm room.

On the way there, Shavon introduces Kashmere to everyone in sight. Loving the attention, but trying not to show it, Kashmere keeps a straight face and continues to walk knowing he's smiling inside all the time. Finally making it to her room, he makes himself comfortable by lounging across her bed. Her phone begins to ring.

"Hello?" she answers.

"Hey Shavon, can I speak to Kashmere, this is Rodney," he says as she hands over the phone.

"Hello."

"Yo, we at the Hyatt Hotel in suite 210 and 211. Just come to 210 to get your key," Rodney said.

"Aiight, yo, I'll be there in a couple of hours."

"Aiight."

"Aiight," he responds hanging the phone up.

"So what was he talking about?" Shavon asks.

"Nothing, he was just telling me my room number," he responds as he lies back across the bed.

The next couple of hours, Kashmere sees the most half naked women in one day that he's ever seen, and some don't even pay him any attention. But it is two girls in particular that really stand out. These two girls, twins to be exact, literally don't care. They came into Shavon's room in just bras and thongs. They sit down and talk with Kashmere for at least two hours while Shavon goes to practice and two of her classes. They both are 5'2", 135 lbs, have light green eyes with caramel skin and banging bodies. Within these two hours Kashmere finds out their names are Jyia and Nyia, that they are 21 with Jyia being the oldest by two minutes. Also that they are from DC and both are single.

"So how long have you known Shavon? And are ya'll together?" Jyia curiously asked.

"For like almost a year. Naw, we not together we just real good friends."

"Did ya'll ever sleep together? Now be truthful 'cause she will tell me anyhow?" Jiya questions not holding back.

"Naw, we don't roll like that, well I can say I don't roll like that with her. I can't speak for her, though," he responds laughing.

"Oh really… you know we be going home almost every other weekend if you want some new friends," Jyia throws in with a low seductive voice.

"Hey it's cool to be friends."

"Aiight" she replies as she gets down her address and phone number in DC and at school. Another thirty minutes passes and Shavon finally arrives back to her room to find Kashmere fast asleep alone, stretched across her bed.

Not waking him, she gets out of her sweaty practice clothes and jumps into the shower. Still in deep slumber, Kashmere lays there not knowing Shavon is in total nude looking for something to put on. When she finishes getting dressed she runs out to grab something to eat for the both of them. Returning back to her room, she finds Kashmere wrapped in a towel lotioning his body.

"Ummm, you look good!" Shavon says.

"Oh, shit! Girl, you scared me!" he says slipping on his boxers and shorts.

"Damn, my bad, I got you something to eat."

"Oh aiight. Some dude named Lamar called, he sounded mad 'cause I picked up the phone," Kashmere said. "I told him I was your cousin, then he calmed down."

"Oh aiight. That's my man crazy ass, let me call him," she replies picking up the phone.

They start to argue as soon as Lamar picks up While they argue, Kashmere sits quietly watching TV and eating.

"That's my cousin!" she screams out. "No I'm not fucking him," she adds as Kashmere snatches the phone.

"Look, yo, you going to stop screamin' on my l'il cousin? Don't worry about me 'cause I won't be here anyways. So calm that 'what you fucking that nigga' young shit up… Damn, she can't have a family visit?" Kashmere screams.

"If she was fucking me do you think she would tell me to answer the phone if it rings, knowing you may call. Think about that shit… Now, apologize to her. Nice talking with you…bro," he concludes handing the phone back, leaving Lamar in total silence.

After ten minutes Shavon gets off the phone.

"So what's up?"

"Nothing, he apologized and we going to the movies. Thank you," she says hugging him.

"No problem… Don't let no nigga yell at you like that no more either," he says. "I'm serious, you better than that."

"OK," she replies.

"What's up with these strip joints? You got somebody to take me down there, 'cause I doubt if Rodney's going tonight; he tied up with shorty."

At that moment the phone rang. "Hello?" Shavon answers.

"Where's my boy?"

"Speaking of the devil. Hey, Rodney, you need to come back so ya'll can go to the strip joint."

Not saying a word, Rodney quickly hangs up.

"Damn, he just hung up!" Shavon said laughing.

"So who going to take us?"

"My girls Jyia and Nyia who were in here earlier." She says. "They work down at the 'Gentlemen's Club.' Oh aiight, I'll see," she says opening the door. "I'll be right back."

While she goes down to the twins' room, Rodney and Dejah enter the room laughing.

"Hey, boy," Dejah says as she goes into the bathroom.

"Yo, I got a rental so are you ready?" Rodney asks.

"When you get that?" Kashmere replied.

"When me and Dejah left earlier, she took me to the spot where she knew somebody," Rodney explained. "So what's up, we still going?"

"Yeah, Shavon's friends work at the club so we going with them… They some sexy ass twins," Kashmere says with a devilish smile.

"For real, what's up with them?" Rodney inquired.

The next ten minutes, Kashmere explains how they look, where they're from and whatever Rodney asks.

Fifteen minutes later, Shavon along with the twins enter the room. Filled with shock, Rodney stares at the twins without speaking a word.

"Are ya'll ready?" Jyia asks talking to Kashmere.

"Yeah, but let me introduce you to my boy, Rodney," he starts to say.

"Rodney, this is Jyia and Nyia."

Still not saying a word, Rodney sits there quietly as they all wait for him to respond.

"Oh my bad, damn, I'm ready." Rodney finally says something.

"We'll be right behind you, is that aiight?"

"I got a better idea, how about you ride with my sister and Kashmere rides with me?" Jyia suggests not noticing how Shavon's looking at her.

Just before they can walk out the door, Shavon grabs Jyia and tells everyone to go to the car and wait. Five minutes later Jyia runs out and jumps in the car.

"Everything aiight?" Kashmere questions.

"Yeah, she just was asking me was I trying to get with you?"

"Oh for real, and what you say to her?" Kashmere inquires.

"I told her the truth, that I was interested and if she was also she needed to let me know." She explains as they turn into the parking lot of the Club. "She says she was just looking out for a good friend. Now hurry up so me and Nyia can get ya'll in."

Following what he was told, Kashmere checks himself in the mirror and joins Rodney and the girls. Once past the security they walk through the club to this exclusive room where only the entertainers were allowed.

"Ya'll lucky, you need big cash to be in this room. But I like ya'll." Jyia says laughing while Kashmere and Rodney take their seats as Nyia sends a waitress for their orders.

"Well, we'll see you two later, we got to go get dressed," Jyia says as she and Nyia head downstairs. The following five hours fly by fast, and Kashmere along with Rodney have seen about twenty different beautiful females.

Almost thirty minutes until closing, Jyia and Nyia enter the room and quickly jump on for a lap dance. When the club closes the owner enters the room and tells the two girls to lock up.

"OK, pop, we'll do that," Jyia responds.

"If ya'll drink something or mess something up, clean it up," he says closing the door leading to the VIP room. On one side Nyia and Rodney explore each others horizons as Jyia and Kashmere count her tips.

"Your boy's nasty," Jyia says laughing.

"I guess your girl is a little angel?" Kashmere says laughing.

"Whateva."

"You know freaks hang together," he says looking at her from the corner of his eyes as he counts the money.

"I know, look at you and Rodney."

"Naw, I was talking about you and Nyia."

As he says that they both start to laugh. They decide to leave the room because the sexual moans are getting louder and louder. Allowing Rodney and Nyia to do their thing, they decide to catch up on the getting to know each other conversation as they head back towards Spellman. When they finally return to Spellman, Kashmere runs up to Shavon's room to say goodbye before heading to his hotel room. Only he finds her wide awake.

"So were the fuck you been 'cause the club been closed."

"You better tell Rodney to go ahead 'cause you staying here," Shavon said with an attitude.

"What? I was at the club helping."

Before he can finish, Shavon finds Rodney's number and calls him, letting him know to go ahead, and that Dejah was also on her way because Shavon was kicking her ass out.

"Now back to you, Mr. Kashmere," she says as she locks the door behind Deja.

"What?"

"So, what you think you're going to screw her half of the morning, then I won't say nothing?"

"What are you talking about, Rodney and Nyia were the ones screwing around… Jyia and me was counting money."

"Whateva, we'll see," Shavon says as she dials the twins' room.

An hour passes, thirty minutes of her talking to Jyia and the other thirty she spends apologizing to Kashmere, knowing now that she made a mistake.

The rest of the week soars by quickly. Kashmere and Rodney are lounging up in the living room. When Kashmere checks his messages, he has ten from Sinsation, five from Stacey and about twenty from Dayshanae with all them questioning his whereabouts. Erasing the messages, he ignores them all.

Letting Rodney out, Kashmere heads straight for his bedroom where he plans to get some sleep. Knowing that someone will call, he decides to turn off the ringer and lies deep under his many blankets.

Chapter eight

Three loud bangs at the front door wakes Kashmere, startling him, causing him to jump instantly to his feet. Dashing down to the front door he finds Sinsation standing there patiently.

"You must be crazy, banging on my door like that," Kashmere says rubbing his eyes, adjusting to the light.

"Where you been?" she questions.

"Out of town, why?" he answers with an attitude. He walks away from the door allowing her to enter. "Why are you so worried?"

"'Cause I was looking for you. I missed you!"

"Whateva, so what's up?" he quickly ignores her and changes the subject.

She lounges around for most of the day, still questioning his whereabouts. After seven hours, she finally quits and heads home. Not giving into her every demand, Kashmere sits quietly listening to some new music playing on the radio. He suddenly recieves a disturbing phone call from Dayshanae's mother.

"Hello," he answers.

"Hey, Kashmere, how you been?" The soft sweet, but broken tearful voice questions.

"Fine, who is this?"

"Ms. Brenda, Dayshanae's mom."

"Hey, ma, how you been? What's going on? You still pimping those men?" Kashmere inquires while laughing, not knowing the true purpose of the call.

"I'm not doing that well," she responds starting to cry again.

"What's wrong? Do you need anything?" he asks as he sits upright, giving her his full attention.

The next twenty-five minutes casually creep by as Ms. Brenda explains the tragedy that happened earlier in the day.

"Dayshanae lost control of her car on the beltway causing it to ram into a guard rail, throwing her through the windshield, directly into the side wall, Kashmere! Come, meet me at the hospital! University in the ICU, hurry she's having surgery as we speak."

"I'm on my way, ma!" Kashmere says, hanging up the phone.

Tears start rolling down his face as he instantily falls to his knees. After at least ten minutes, he grabs his coat and drives as fast as he can.

The minute he arrives, he is greeted by Ms. Brenda and Dayshanae's little sister Kandis. While comforting both of them, Kashmere wipes their eyes and tries to disguise that he's wiping his own also. Kashmere questions every doctor that comes past out of the ICU.

Fourteen hours goes by and the doctor finally allows the three of them to come into recovery for only a few moments. As Kashmere looks down on Dayshanae's disfigured face and body he feels like he just wants to cry but he can't let her see him that upset.

One leg and both her arms are broken, a fractured skull, a ruptured chest and a load of cuts and bruises. She's in a coma, and has all kinds of machines hooked up to her to the point that it's scary. Everyone just cries since there are only family members there. The doctor allows them all to stay until she wakes up, then they would have to alternate.

Five days pass with still no response or movement. Kashmere sat with Dayshanae every minute, holding her hand, praying every minute. Thinking Ms. Brenda is asleep, he begins to talk to Dayshanae, hoping she can hear every word.

Not noticing that Ms. Brenda is standing close behind him, Kashmere starts to reminisce about the first day they met. The days they hung out together and how he felt that God brought them back together for a reason.

Then Kashmere went into a deep silence while tears drenched his face. Suddenly he shares his true feelings about her, how he truly and deeply loves Dayshanae. Then Ms. Brenda places her hand on his shoulder. When Kashmere looks up, a smile appears on Ms. Brenda's face.

"My mother always said this would happen one day," she said squeezing him in a tight hug.

"Ms. Brenda, I love Dayshanae with all my heart and I can't lose her now. I never got a chance to tell her how much she means to me."

The moment he says that Dayshanae begins to make some slight movements. As Kashmere looks over at her she gives a sweet smile and replies, "I love you, too, Kashmere."

Silence falls over the room while Kashmere, along with her sister and mom, hug her softly.

The days following her being awake, Kashmere sat by her side attending to her every need, allowing Ms. Brenda and Kandis to return home for work and school. He spent every waking hour with her for almost a month and a half.

Finally, Dayshanae was laying in her own bed with Kashmere still by her side. The first couple of days back home Dayshanae was visited by old friends, ex-boyfriends and even a couple of her enemies. Neither Kashmere nor Dayshanae knew how far the information of her accident was out on the streets, but they both were shocked when Sinsation walked in with some flowers and a get well card. Sinsation sets down the flowers and card.

"Are you OK, girl?" Sinsation asks like there wasn't an incident between the three of us almost a month ago.

"Yeah, I'm aiight, and you?" Dayshanae calmly asks.

"That's good, and how about you, Kashmere, how are you?"

"I'm cool. Why, what's up?" He responds to Sinsation wondering what she is up to.

"Excuse me, if ya'll think this is rude, but Kashmere, can I talk to you for a quick minute outside, please?" she asks while heading for the front door. Kashmere lets Sinsation wait while he continues to tend to Dayshanae and quickily calls work to inform them of the situation and that he probably wouldn't be returning anytime soon. Finally, he heads outside.

"What's up?" Kashmere asks sitting down on the front steps.

"So, you back with this bitch, huh? What, I wasn't good enough or something?"

"Get out of here with your shit! Coming over here, trying to start something? That's my best friend and I will always be in her life, by her side. If I recall correctly I don't fuck with you anymore, remember? Why would you be worried if I was fucking her in the first place?"

"'Cause I figured we was going to be able to work things out between us, but I guess that is not so. I'm gonna leave now, just tell Dayshanae I said I hope she recovers soon and that the better woman won."

"Get out of here with that crap."

Sinsation walked back to her car very sadly.

"Oh aiight, I can do that for you," he responds not really worried about what she said. Kashmere stays outside to make sure Sinsation leaves 'cause he didn't want a recurring problem like before. Just before he re-enters the house, Kashmere's phone began to ring, showing Rodney's number on the ID.

"What's up cuzin?" he asks

"Ain't nothing; what's going on?" Rodney says.

"Dayshanae had an accident."

"What! She ok?"

"Yeah, now, but it was touch and go for a while."

"What happened?"

"I will tell you when I see you 'cause I'm with her now and I don't want to upset her talking about it."

"Ok, hit me up when you leave," Rodney said.

"Bet!" said Kashmere.

"Hey, look, that Danna and Stacey wanted to hook-up."

Just the mention of their names brought Kashmere to tell Rodney about all the messages she had left on his machine while they were in Georgia.

"For real, yo, I had a lot of messages from shorty, too," Kashmere says. "So what they talking about doing?"

"Shit, I don't know, but I'm coming over there to see how Dayshanae is and we can talk when I get there," Rodney says.

"Oh, aiight, then see you when you get here," Kashmere responds as he heads back to Dayshanae's room. As soon as he reaches her room he tells her that Rodney was coming to see her.

"What his crazy ass want?" She inquires.

"To see you and how you're doing. I told him what happened and so he just wanted to come check up on you. Plus he wants to go out later."

"What, to see some shorties, huh?" She says smiling. "Ya'll pimps."

"Whateva, but yeah, some shorties we met when we were at Dave and Busters."

"For real, if you go out again bring me a plate… and wash your shit real good if you get some ass, 'cause I know how you get down," she responds laughing.

"Whateva, girl… I'll make sure I forget your plate, too, since you so-call know me," he responds also laughing.

A few minutes later, Rodney pops his head in the doorway.

"Now who fucked you up? I told you stop trying to be Superwoman or Ms. Dave Earnhart," he shouts as they all laugh.

"Fuck you, Rodney."

"But naw, as long as you aiight, shorty."

"Thank you, smart ass."

"See, that's why I try not to be sincere to your punkass," he quickly reponds causing them to laugh again.

"So, what tramps ya'll chillin with tonight?" Dayshanae asks being nosey. "Just make sure if ya'll go eat that Kashmere brings me a plate."

"I'll see, nosey ass… but why they got to be tramps? That's not nice. They are, but damn, that's still not nice," Rodney says laughing but being a little serious.

"See ya'll two triflings."

"Hold up I didn't even say shit….so why I got to be a trifling?" Kashmere quickly defends himself.

"Whateva, you and Rodney just alike, trifling dawgs," Dayshanae says laughing. "Don't ya'll got a date or something?"

"Yeah we do, but that's amazing how I'm a trifling dawg but you still want me," Kashmere says laughing as he and Rodney walk towards the front door.

They don't instantly leave right away; they sit and talk outside for a couple of minutes about their plans and about what happened to Dayshanae.

"So what's up, yo? Did you talk to them?" Kashmere questions.

"Oh yeah, they're going to meet us at Dave and Busters in like two hours."

Once that's said, they part their ways for home to change clothes.

"I'll be at your crib when I get dressed," Rodney says. He pulls up beside Kashmere just before Kashmere can get into his car.

"Aiight, cuzin," Kashmere replies stepping into his car.

Waiting at home for Rodney, Kashmere sits in darkness, lounging across his couch listening to music. During his time alone he wonders about his past relationship problems and his future. Then Rodney walks in.

"Damn, why the fuck you're sitting in the dark for? Turn some fucking lights on. Damn!" he shouts out as he flicks the switch to find Kashmere on the couch.

"You ready, yo?" Rodney asks.

"Yeah, let's go."

On the 295 beltway they both lie back and relax calmly as the smooth, soothing voice of Alicia Keys rings through the air. Stopping at the gas station right before Dave and Busters, they fill the tank and continue on their way not noticing the girls have pulled in right behind. They jump out and head to the front door when suddenly a car races up and instantly stops, scaring the living hell out of them both.

"What the fuck is you doing?" Kashmere yells.

"Dumbass DC niggas!" Rodney shouts out as the hazard lights come on and the door opens.

"Do we look like some dumb ass DC niggas to you?" Danna questions.

"I told her not to do that dumb shit, you OK?" Stacey says as she grabs Kashmere close to her and kisses his neck. "You OK?" She asks again.

"Yeah, I'm aiight," Kashmere answers, returning the hug.

During their little romantic moment, Rodney and Danna play fight, causing themselves to tire out.

"So what we going to do?" Kashmere questions.

"I thought we were going to eat?"

"Naw, we just wanted ya'll to meet us here. We all going back to my place. I cooked," Danna says pushing Rodney into her car.

"We'll be right behind you," Kashmere replies as he opens the door for Stacy while he laughs at Rodney getting man-handled.

On the way to Danna's, Kashmere sits and listens to Stacey explain how she missed him while he was gone. Deep in thought about Dayshanae's wellbeing, Kashmere ignores every word that leaves Stacey's mouth.

At Danna's, Kashmere and Stacey lounge across the couch while, as usual, Rodney has departed to the bedroom with Danna.

"She's going to put a hurting on your boy," Stacey says laughing.

"You must got him confused, that's my peoples and we the one's who put the hurting on our victims," Kashmere responds with a devilish smirk across his face.

"Nigga, whateva, neither one of ya'll is about shit, ya'll just all mouth."

Not responding right away, Kashmere sits quietly allowing her to hear how Danna is screaming out Rodney's name.

"Well I see you got the dick look on your face, 'cause it don't sound like she is putting a hurting on a damn thing. On the other hand she hurting the shit out of his ears along with the neighbors' ears," Kashmere says leaning back across the couch.

"Whateva, that's your boy, not you."

"Hey you the one full of shit," he responds sitting up.

"As bad as I want to I can't… I just came on my period."

"Hold up, you talking all this shit and you can't do shit? Like I said before, full of shit."

"How you figure that?"

"Look at all the shit you talking and then you tell me you're on your period," he starts to explain. "Now switch this shit around what you think?"

"OK, I see your point. I'm sorry, I should have told you from the jump."

"It's aiight, it ain't that serious," Kashmere responds lying back, grabbing the TV remote.

Minutes after they finish, Rodney and Danna enter the living room to find Kashmere along with Stacey deep in slumber on opposite ends of the couch.

"Wake up, nigga!" Rodney yells, startling Kashmere and causing him to hop up to his feet.

"What, yo?"

"Let's go, bring your ass on," Rodney says giving his last hug to Danna. Then he walks to the car.

The whole ride home Rodney tells Kashmere the whole situation, from the car ride to Danna's and the physical encounter in the bedroom.

Instead of going home, Kashmere heads for Dayshanae's. When he gets there he ends his conversation with Rodney and returns to the aid of Dayshanae. When he reaches her room he stands in the doorway for a couple of minutes just watching how peaceful she is sleeping. While he stands there she suddenly wakes up, not allowing him to notice. Then she whispers to him to show that's she's awake.

"So how was your little date?"

"It was aiight, why you still up?" Kashmere questions.

"Why you standing there?" She questions as she looks at him.

"I didn't want to disturb you?"

"Oh, well I was kinda waiting for you," she says. "Come here."

"What's up?" he says as he sits beside her.

"So did you screw that bitch? And I want to know the truth," she asks him in one of her aggressive voices.

"Naw," Kashmere answers.

"Whateva, why not?"

"'Cause she was on….."

"So, if she wasn't, you would of screwed her, huh?" she says sitting up.

"Probably not, 'cause while I was sitting there all I could think of was you."

"Nigga, don't give me that bullshit," Dayshanae responds lying back down.

"Yo, I'm serious." Kashmere turned and leaned over to her. "Look, I'm serious. All I could do was think about you."

"OK, so if you think about me so much, like you say you do, then why the fuck you leave me here and go to her…? 'Cause you thought you were going to get some ass?" she turned her back to him. "If I was that so-called important, your ass would've stayed."

"Look…" he starts to say.

"I don't want to hear it, Kashmere, just lie your ass down and go to sleep so you can call Rodney in the morning to come get your ass."

Dayshanae assists him in pulling the covers up to return to sleep. Not saying another word, he lies down, not even getting undressed. He lies there and falls fast asleep.

Chapter nine

A week goes by and Kashmere still finds himself on Dayshanae's bad side. The argument has gone so far that she won't return any of his phone calls. Trying not to carry an attitude, he decides to let her calm down by not calling for a couple of days.

The next day, Kashmere receives calls from Sinsation and even Jyia, but still no word from Dayshanae. Deciding to mend their friendship, he heads to her house. When he arrives he notices Ms. Brenda and Dayshanae's grandmother on the porch.

"Oh, if it ain't Mr. 'In the dog house' Kashmere," Ms. Brenda shouts as they all started to laugh.

"Hey ma, Hey grandma!" he greets them with laughter in his voice as he gives them both a hug. Is Dayshanae asleep?"

"No, but we got to talk to you before you go in there," Ms. Brenda said.

"It's that bad?" he questions.

"No, but just sit your butt down and listen so it won't happen again."

For the next twelve minutes the women of the house explain how a woman wants to know everything, but can't always handle everything. How when a woman is in love with a friend she sometimes acts like she doesn't care what that friend does, when really she is heartbroken by every mention of another woman.

"OK, so why do ya'll do that?" Kashmere curiously asks.

"It's human nature, I can't explain it…but you men do it also," Ms. Brenda points out.

"Ya'll sure do," Grandma adds on.

"So, Dayshanae's not really mad, she just feels heartbroken?"

"I see you were paying attention. So in order to fix this, you need to acknowledge her feelings and go from there," Ms. Brenda directs him. "Because my daughter loves you. I can remember her talking about her crush on you back in Middle school, but you were still the ladies' man that you are now," she adds on.

"Oh, really? Go on, what else did she used to do?" Kashmere urges her on.

"Boy, I already said too much. Take your butt in the house," she responds as they all laugh.

Just before he goes inside he hugs them both again and heads for Dayshanae's room. Sitting quietly, watching her soaps, Dayshanae pays no mind to Kashmere as he enters the room and lies across the bottom of the bed. After a couple of minutes he notices that she isn't going to say anything so he tries to start up a conversation.

"So you not talking to me?" he says tapping her on the leg.

Trying her best to ignore him, Dayshanae continues to watch TV until she is finally annoyed by his repetitive tapping.

"Stop, boy, you getting on my nerves!" she says laughing.

"So you not talking to me?"

"What, boy? What do you want?" Dayshanae yells out still laughing.

"I wanted to apologize for leaving you that night. What can I do to make it up to you?? He says looking in her eyes.

"I got to think about that one," she quickly responds with a devilish smile on her face.

"Get your mind out the gutter," Kashmere says noticing the look on her face.

"Whateva." Forgetting the whole argument Dayshanae lays her head across his chest and continues to watch her soaps. As she watches TV, Kashmere doses off leaving her unaware he's asleep. When the soaps are finally over, she turns to find him fast asleep. Not bothering him, she turns back around and goes to sleep herself. Sleeping the whole day away, night falls quickly over the two, copying a routine out of Kashmere's archives.

Dayshanae finally wakes up and notices how peaceful Kashmere looks while he is sleeping. Following watching him, she finds something to watch on TV and gently rubs her fingertips across his head.

"What's up?" he asks being awakened by the first touch.

"Go back to sleep," she responds as he becomes comfortable laying his head across her lap. While she continues to stroke his soft skin with her fingertips, she slips into a deep thought of how it would be if her and Kashmere were together like her grandmother always predicted. Allowing him to get at least three more hours of sleep, she wakes him just in time for dinner.

"Hey, you… Wake up, it's time to eat," she softly whispers.

"Aiight," he responds looking at her then sitting to fully wake up. "Did Rodney call 'cause I got to get the car."

"Yeah, he said to call him when you wake up. Just call him after you eat. Oh, and your pager has been blowing up, too. I guess you wanted by all your females friends," Dayshanae says handing him his pager.

"You probably called back, knowing you."

"You not my man, why would I call back?"

"That's just you," Kashmere responds laughing.

"Come on, let's go eat or are you eating up here?"

"Up here," she responds lying down.

"Aiight, I'll eat up here with you. I'll be right back."

Downstairs he finds Ms. Brenda and Grandma sitting at the table eating with two extra plates on the table, filled with food.

"Thanks, Ms. Brenda, you must of known we were going to eat upstairs."

"I know she wasn't coming downstairs," she responds.

"Come on, you carry the plates and I'll be nice and carry ya'll drinks," She adds laughing.

"It's Rodney," Dayshanae says handing Kasmere the phone and taking her plate as her mom puts down the drinks and heads back downstairs.

"What's up cuzin?" Kashmere greets him.

"Ain't shit… Yo, I'll be over in a minute 'cause after I drop you off I'm hooking up with this shorty," Rodney explains. "Oh yeah, that crazy broad Sinsation said call her, I saw her at the gas station."

"Aiight, I'll see you when you get here cuzin, I'm about to go eat," Kashmere responds filling his mouth with greens, potatoe salad and fried chicken, then he hangs up the phone. As they both eat, Kashmere's pager goes off.

"See your hoes want you. I told you stop lacing them with that dick of yours… I heard about you," Dayshanae says with a grin on her face.

"Say what? What you hear?" Kashmere questions wondering what was said.

"Huh, I ain't saying nothing."

"Whateva, what did you hear?"

"Nothing really. I just heard you know what you're doing," she responds looking him up and down, biting her bottom lip.

"What's that look for?" Kashmere asks putting his fork down.

"Oh, nothing just thinking about what I was told."

"It makes you bite your lip?"

"Hell, yeah! I mean, yeah…" she responds continuing to bite her lip.

"Now you know you got to tell me now," Kashmere says looking her dead in the face.

"Aiight… Aiight! Damn," Dayshanae says lying back on some pillows.

As he lies back to prepare himself to intake what's been said about him, Dayshanae starts to go in detail, word for word situations that Kashmere's been encountered in, with a certain female. Throwing hints out, not trying to put the person straight out there, Dayshanae continues with her story. Kashmere lies there listening to her every word; he finally figures out who's been running their mouth.

"Sinsation!" he yells out.

"What? What are you talking about?"

"She told you all this shit didn't she?" He questions sitting straight up.

"Yeah, you know that was my friend before the altercation."

"So she been running her mouth?" he says. "So now you curious, huh?"

"Look, I ain't saying all that," Dayshanae responds quickly trying to cover up a small smirk that has appeared on her face.

"Whateva, girl… I see your face," he says as he continues to eat.

"Think what you wanna think 'cause if I was that curious trust me you would know," she adds returning to her own plate.

"Oh I would, huh?"

"Yes, you would," as she says that Rodney walks in carrying a plate filled with chicken.

"What's up, ya'll?" Rodney says with a mouth full of food.

"Ain't shit," Kashmere responds moving over to make room for Rodney to sit down.

While they eat, Kashmere sits quietly still thinking about his recent conversation with Dayshanae. After they eat, Rodney drops Kashmere back at his house so he can change clothes and pick up his car. Just before he can get in the door he hears the phone ring.

"Shit, the phone's ringing!" he mutters to himself as he struggles for the keys. When he enters he leaps for the phone.

"Hello? Hello?" he quickly says as he listens to the dial tone. Not really worried about the call, Kashmere glances at the caller ID and continues on his way to the shower.

While he's in the shower he hears the ringing of the phone off and on. After his shower, the caller ID reads that he has received ten new calls. They were all from a number he didn't recognize, just like the call he missed before his shower. The minute he's dressed he returns the phone call.

"Hello?" a familiar voice answers.

"Yeah, somebody called me?" Kashmere says.

"This is Jyia… How you been?"

"Oh, I'm aiight. This number was messing up my head. So, what's going on?" Kashmere says.

"Nothing, chillin', making money as usual," she responds.

"I hear that."

They talked for hours laughing and joking. She let him know that she and her sister would be in DC in two weeks, and she wanted to chill with him again.

Going on their fourth hour of conversation, Kashmere remembers that he told Dayshanae he was coming back over.

"Oh shit!" he screams.

"What's wrong?" she says in a worried tone.

"I forgot I told my friend I was coming back over. Gimme your number so I can call you back," he answers grabbing a paper and pen. As soon as he gets the number, Kashmere runs out the door. Kashmere finds Dayshanae laid across her bed with a tray filled with food in front of her.

"Damn, that was a long shower," she says in a smart tone.

"I got a phone call from my friend in Atlanta," he replies sitting at the end of the bed.

"Oh, you mean one of your hoes?"

"There you go… I'll be back, I'm about to go get me a plate."

When he returns, Dayshanae is laughing and joking with one of her female friends. Her friend, being a loud person, allows Kashmere to hear every word of her side of the conversation.

"Boy, stop being nosey!" Dayshanae yelled out.

"What are you talking about?" he says, playing dumb.

"Your ass is never quiet and you all of a sudden quiet, stop being nosey!"

"Man, I don't have to take this! I'm going to continue eating my food," he says. "It ain't my fault your girl is loud and ghetto," he smiles.

"Girl, let me call you back when nosey ass ain't around," Dayshanae says hanging up the phone. "Kashmere you a trip."

"Huh? What I do?"

"Nothing…you ain't do nothing," she replies smiling.

"I know," Kashmere mumbles while he returns to his meal and Dayshanae calls to her mom for seconds.

"Girl, get your ass up, you big baby!"

"Shut up, I don't feel like it," she responds as she continues to call for her mom. After she shouts a good five times, her mom finally strolls in, grabs the plate and returns in five minutes with it full.

"Damn, you sure is eating a lot, are you pregnant?" Kashmere asks when her mom disappears.

"Hell, no… I'm not pregnant! You didn't screw me yet," she says in a mumble, smiling.

"What you say?" Kashmere says catching bits and pieces of what was just said. "Did you say I didn't screw you yet?"

"Huh? No I didn't say that, but if I did?" Dayshanae says glancing at him.

"You said you didn't say it, so it shouldn't matter what I would of said."

"Tell me what you would of said."

"Why, you said you didn't say it, right?" Kashmere says looking at her smiling.

"Look, you know I said it, so tell me," Dayshanae says frustrated.

"So why you tell me you didn't say it? Just for lying I'm still not telling you," he says laughing, knowing he's hit a nerve.

"Stop playing, tell me."

"Truthfully, I don't know, let me think on it."

"Whateva, Kashmere," she replies as her phone begins to ring.

Noticing who it is, Kashmere tells her that he'll be back in a couple of hours. Before leaving, he drops his plate off in the kitchen and heads back to his house.

At his house, Kashmere decides to give Jyia a call back only to find out that she has her cell phone off. So he pages her so that they can finish their conversation from earlier that day. Five minutes later Kashmere's found laid back across his couch laughing and joking with Jyia like before.

Within an hour of talking, Jyia informs him of her and her sister's exact date for coming to DC. She also says how much she enjoyed him when they chilled the first time and would love to see him again.

"That's cool with me," Kashmere says. "Just hit me when ya'll get here and I'll let Rodney know, too, for your sister."

"Aiight, I'll do that… So I'll talk to you when I get to DC," Jyia responds just before they say their goodbyes then hang up.

Ka'Shus

Chapter ten

It's three days before the twins are supposed to be in DC. Kashmere is lounging across the couch waiting on Rodney to come over so they can go out to grab something to eat. The minute he gets comfortable watching the Cartoon Network there's a knock on the door.

"Yo, it's open!" he yells out, not wanting to move. Instead of Rodney strolling in, Sinsation walks in making her presence known.

"You shouldn't leave your door open like that, just anybody can walk in your house," she says closing the door behind her.

"I thought you were Rodney. What the fuck are you doing here?" He questions standing to his feet.

"I just wanted to stop by for a visit. Damn, I can't see how you're doing?"

"For what, I don't like people poppin up at my shit, you should've called first."

"I did a couple of times, but you didn't answer, and I saw your car out front so I stopped by," she says, explaining her side of the story.

"OK, maybe I didn't feel like being bothered. That's why I didn't pick up the phone. I do have caller ID," Kashmere responds giving her the dumb face.

Just before Sinsation can answer, the phone begins to ring. As Kashmere answers the phone, Sinsation continues with the conversation.

"Hello?" he asks raising one finger to try to shut her up.

"Hey, boy, what's up" Dayshanae says.

"Nothing chillin', what's up with you, boo?" he replies.

When Sinsation hears the word 'Boo' she begins to show her ass, yelling and screaming. Ignoring her, Kashmere continues on with his conversation.

"So what's going on?" He asked.

"Who is that?"

"That's Sinsation with her dumb ass, she's about to leave," he responds opening the door.

"What, now you messing with her again, phoney bitch. I don't care about anybody else but that bitch… I hate that phoney bitch," she screams.

"I didn't know she…." Kashmere starts to say before Dayshanae continues her argument cutting him off.

"I don't want to hear shit you got to say! Fuck you and her!" she says slamming down the phone.

"Hello… Hello?" he repeats as he hangs up to redial her number.

"Who was that?" Sinsation asks.

"Dayshanae, why?"

"You going to call her ass back while I'm standing right here… You just going to disrespect me like that?" She yells out.

Filled with frustration, he shouts out the first thing that pops in his head.

"BITCH, I'm not disrespecting nobody… Your ass wasn't invited in the first place… So leave, BITCH!"

"BITCH? BITCH? Who the fuck you calling a BITCH?" She yells charging towards him swinging.

Watching her every swing, he gives her a slight push which causes her to fall back hitting her head on the glass table. She lies there, feeling the blood seep out her head slowly. "I'm bleeding… Oh, you fucked up now."

"Hey, you brought it upon yourself, I just pushed you," Kashmere responds continuosly dialing to get through to Dayshanae.

Not paying him any mind, Sinsation grabs her cell phone and calls the police claiming Kashmere beat her up.

Ten minutes later, the block is filled with patrol cars. Ignoring the sirens, 'cause he's used to hearing them, Kashmere continues to explain the situation to Dayshanae.

After seeing the blood from Sinsation's head, the police proceed to apprehend Kashmere. Walking straight in the open door the officer approaches Kashmere.

"Mr. Kashmere?"

"Hold on, Dayshanae. Yes, sir, I'm Kashmere."

"You're under arrest."

"For what?" Kashmere questions.

"For the beating of the young lady outside."

Looking out the doorway, Kashmere spots Sinsation in tears talking to the police. "I didn't hit that girl."

"OK, well she said you did, we can talk about it on the way to the station," the officer replies reaching out for him.

"Dayshanae, meet me down at central booking. This bitch said I beat her up."

"What? Stop playing!" Dayshanae shouts. "Aiight, I'll be there."

The minute he's off the phone the officer escorts him to the car, while Sinsation continues with her show.

"I told you, don't fuck with me, Kashmere," Sinsation says with a smirk, not allowing the police to see.

As they put him in the car, Rodney pulls up and spots Kashmere in cuffs.

"What the fuck's going on?" He shouts out racing towards the situation.

"Mr. Kashmere is under arrest for the beating of this young lady," the officer says pointing at Sinsation.

"Man, that phoney Bitch? My peoples ain't hit her."

"Well she said he did, so we're going downtown to talk about it."

"Yo, I'll be down there... did you call Dayshanae?" Rodney asks.

Kashmere is now in the back of the car and shakes his head 'yes' as they pull off towards central booking.

After an hour of arguing and convincing, Kashmere is released on bail.

Finally, calmed down and back home, Kashmere along with Rodney and Dayshanae sit talking about what they're going to do about Sinsation.

"I say we beat the bitch ass," Rodney says.

"What, so she can call the police again and have you and Kashmere both yellow asses in jail?" Dayshanae responds. "Plus beating her ass isn't going to change anything."

"True... Truthfully, I don't give a fuck. That's what she wants us to do, is to worry."

"Fuck, it's what goes around comes around," Kashmere says pulling his shirt over his head.

"Yo, just forget about it."

Chapter eleven

Still a little stressed out, Kashmere and Rodney are at Foxy's Playground in DC watching the twins do their thing.

"Yo, Jyia is doing her thing," Kashmere says drinking his Henne and coke.

"I know, Nyia is too… I'm going to have to dig in that tonight," Rodney replies laughing. "You need to stop bullshitting and get down with Jyia. She is literally throwing her shit to you," he adds on.

"How you figure that?"

"Yo, she called from Atlanta and said she wanted to see you, right? She keeps looking over here, just try and see what happens, aiight?" Rodney suggests.

"Aiight, we'll see."

When the club finally closes, they grab something to eat and end up back at the twins' hotel room. Knowing in advance that Kashmere and Rodney are coming, Jyia and Nyia got separate rooms. Not wasting time, Rodney and Nyia begin struggling to get in the room. On the other hand, Kashmere and Jyia casually walk in the room, talking about recent incidents.

"Damn, you fuck with them crazy bitches! See," Jyia says as she gets undressed to get in the shower.

"Everybody says that I can't help it, that seems to be all that's attracted to me."

"I'm not crazy…yet," Jyia responds laughing.

"See, that's how they always start off, calm and easy. Then they start flippin' out."

"Stop slinging that thing of yours," she responds, stepping inside the shower.

"Whateva, I can't help that either!" Kashmere yells loud enough for her to hear him as he flips through the TV channels.

After her shower she sits down beside Kashmere while she lotions her body.

"So you like them insane bitches, huh?" Jyia asks laughing.

"Forget you, girl."

"Don't get mad… The poor baby," She continues to mess with him.

"Keep on here," Kashmere says laughing.

"Aiigh, Aiight… I'll stop. So, other than that what's going on? Did you miss me?" she quickly slides in as she slips on her boxers and baby tee.

"Yeah, I missed you… Yeah, a-huh" he responds being sarcastic.

"Whateva, boy, dump my money out of my bag for me so we can count it up, please."

"You about to pay me for my services," Kashmere says laughing, dumping out her bag.

"I'll pay you, aiight," Jyia replies with a sexy smile.

"Whateva you say," he says, not really paying her any mind.

Not adding onto the ignored subject, they continue to sort the money from ones, fives, twenties and even a couple of fifty's and hundreds. After they finish counting all her earnings, they set up and watch some lame ass love story.

Once again, not engaging in anything physical, Jyia and Kashmere rudly wake up Rodney and Nyia to go grab some breakfast from IHOP's.

While they wait for their food, the girls need to go to the bathroom. As soon as they are out of sight, Rodney begins his story about last night.

"Yo, last night shorty Nyia, was off the hook, she sucked the rooster like it was the last blow-pop on earth," he says grabbing himself. "Yo, my damn toes curled the fuck up. She needs to train some of these B'More broads," he adds as they both start to laugh.

"Yo, cuzin, you crazy," Kashmere says laughing.

"Did you hit up Jyia yet?"

"Naw yo, I didn't even try, yo. I was just chillin'," Kashmere starts drinking his orange juice.

"Cuzin, she is waiting to throw that stuff on you. Her sister said that Jyia feels like you don't even want her."

"Yo, it ain't like…." Kashmere begins to say when the females sit down, instantly ending their conversation.

A second before their food arrives, Kashmere's pager starts buzzing, showing Dayshanae's number with 911 after it around three times. He instantly pulls out his cell to call her.

"What's wrong?" He asks worried.

"Nothing, I just was worried 'cause I haven't talked to you."

"Girl don't do that I was worried as hell… I'm aiight. I'm in DC with Rodney and the twins.

"Oh damn, you did tell me you were going there but I forgot it was this weekend. My bad, I'll just see you when you get back home. OK, bye," Dayshanae says hanging up, not giving him a chance to respond or say bye.

"Who was that cuzin?" Rodney questions as the waitress places their plates in front of them.

"Dayshanae."

As soon as Kashmere says her name Jyia gives her sister a look that sends her a message about their earlier conversation in the bathroom.

"I'm not going to bite my tongue, 'cause that's not me. Is that the reason you won't fuck me?" Jyia inquires as the couple next to them drops their forks in shock.

"Huh?" Kashmere responds being caught off guard by the question.

"I said is she the reason you won't screw me?"

"Naw… I just was trying to chill and I really didn't know what you were all about," he responds covering himself.

"Well to put it out there, I want to fuck you. No, excuse me, I want to fuck the shit out of you. Now the ball is in your court," Jyia says. "That's the end of that conversation. We'll find out tonight if you want me or not," she adds continuing to eat her food.

"Yeah, I guess we'll see," Kashmere says looking at Rodney.

"And you better screw the shit out of her, too," Rodney says, instigating the situation.

"I know, that's right! I second, third, and fourth that motion," Jyia says making them all laugh.

Since Jyia asked that question she kept her eyes on Kashmere every second she could get. Now back in the room, Jyia put her boxers and tee on not planning to leave no time soon. But Kashmere on the other hand, heads directly to the shower. Facing the wall, with water racing down his head and back, he sits quietly deep in thought as Jaheim plays blasting on the stereo.

With the music flooding out the sound of the opening of the door, Jyia creeps in. For a minute, she watches in ambition trying to tame the inner lust that surges through her body. She quietly undresses and steps into the back of the shower. Still deep in thought, Kashmere doesn't realize that Jyia has joined him. Without a word, Jyia glides her nails softly down Kashmere's back. He jumps up, surprised that he's not alone anymore.

"Are you OK?" she whispers as she rubs his freshly shaven head.

"Yeah, I'm aiight just trying to relax…alone."

"Oh, what? Am I bothering you?" she responds removing her hand from his body.

"Naw, but I was just trying to relax," he answers, not noticing that she has already stormed out the door.

Finishing his shower, he walks in the room to find Jyia sitting on the edge of the bed with her head hanging down. Standing right in front of her in his boxers and wife beater he looks down on her.

"What's wrong wit you?"

"Nuttin, I'm in my relax mood," she says copying what he was saying in the shower.

"Oh aiight," he responds as he begins to walk away.

"But I didn't say I wanted to be alone," Jyia quickly says grabbing his legs while she starts to kiss his thighs upward towards the staff of pleasure that she's been waiting to feel.

With Kashmere inching away, she gently pulls down his boxers. Her eyes spread wide open at the sight of how his satisfaction tool is hung and hooked. Before Kashmere can gain the energy to resist, she hurries and licks across the head of the hook. That sends a sensual surge shooting straight up his back, paralyzing Kashmere's every move.

Under her spell of temptation, Kashmere glides his fingers through her hair as she swallows every inch of his manhood. Slowly Jyia tastes the smooth caramel coated skin that covers Kashmere from head to toe. Deeper into exctasy, he stops her at his chest and lays her across the bed. His tongue swirls around the tiny nudget tip found deep between the lips that surround the opening to the tunnel of her everlasting bliss, that is urging to be released.

While the exotic four play game continues it quickly becomes a scene of imagination leading Jyia to show her riding skills as she pretends to be the lone ranger. Kashmere decides to show his qualifications in this field.

After hours of sweat flying, nails digging and orgasms pouring, they both lie exhausted from the workout.

"Damn, if I knew it was like that I would have jumped on it," Jyia says continuing to look him up and down.

"What you mean?"

"I mean, you know what you're doing."

"Oh, aiight…you do, too, kinda-sorta," he responds laughing.

"What you mean kinda-sorta?" Jyia says looking a bit confused.

"Girl, calm down! You aiight…look at you all on the defensive side," he responds laughing at how she's acting.

"I'm not worried about it, I know I did my thing. I need a couple of hours to sleep before I go dance tonight," Jyia says laying on the bed.

"I hear that…. That's the best idea you ever had other than wanting me," Kashmere replies as they both laugh.

"Boy, shut up you are crazy. Lay your ass down, you need some sleep 'cause you acting up."

"Whateva."

Chapter twelve

Going on a week from his sexual incident with Jyia, Kashmere can't even make a phone call because if he picks up the phone Jyia always seems to be on the other end. Not seeing or talking to Dayshanae, he decides to stop trying to call her. He heads straight to her house to show that he is OK with no cuts or bruises.

"Hey, you sick sexy thaaang, you!" Kashmere shouts out to Dayshanae who's sitting on the front porch.

"Oh, now you decide to come see me.... I heard you've been back for at least a week. Why didn't you come straight here like you usually do?" Dayshanae questions crossing her arms. "What, you had to get rid of all the pussy juices and smells?"

"See, a nigga stops by to show you he's aiight and you flip out on him as usual. Where's mommy? I know she'll be happy to see me, even grandma would be happy," Kashmere responds walking by her, not even giving her a hug or anything.

"Hey momma, what's you cooking?" He shouts walking in the house as Dayshanae decides to follow.

On his route to the kitchen, Kashmere is cut off by a tug on his shirt pulling him towards the stairs leading to Dayshanae's room. Snatching his shirt away, he continues his mission to the kitchen being lead by the smell of food being cooked.

"I'm telling your mother, don't try to stop me now… Hey momma!" he continues to yell out.

"What Kashmere? Your plate is almost ready. Once I heard your voice I knew what you were coming for," Ms. Brenda says hugging him.

"Thank you…. You do care, other than grandma… To bad I can't say the same thing about your sorry daughter," He says laughing with Dayshanae right behind him.

"Hey, where's grandma anyways?"

"Upstairs asleep; she just went to bed," Ms. Brenda answers handing Kashmere his over-piled plate.

"Thank you, ma…. Excuse me," Kashmere says nudging by Dayshanae, heading for her room. "Oh yeah, hey Dayshanae, get me something to drink…. Thank you!" he shouts from halfway up the stairs. In her room, Kashmere is lounging across her bed eating his food.

"Boy, you better get your shoes off my bed…here," Dayshanae says passing him his drink aggressively.

"Thank you."

Right before Dayshanae sits down her phone begins to ring.

"Oh Lord," Kashmere mumbles after answering she hands him the phone.

"It's for you…it's a girl name Danielle,"

"Who? I don't know no damn Danielle," he responds taking the phone. "Hello?"

Being on the phone for only five minutes he drops his fork and the phone and races out the house leaving Dayshanae in a state of shock. She picks up the phone and talks to Danielle to find out what's going on. Only a minute into the conversation, a tear rolls down Dayshanae's face.

After they are done talking, Dayshanae screams for her mother. Her mother comes running to her aid.

"What's wrong? What's wrong? Her mother says repeatedly.

"Rodney got killed!" Dayshanae screams hugging her mother and crying.

"Where's Kashmere?" Mama asks.

"I don't know, he just stormed out the door. I hope he's not doing anything stupid," Dayshanae says wiping her eyes.

Kashmere was speeding down the street crazy. His heart was beating uncontrollably; he was even having problems with his breathing. He imagined everything, not exactly knowing what had happened. Maybe Rodney wasn't dead at all, maybe Danielle made a mistake, and maybe he was just hurt really bad.

Finally arriving, Kashmere sees Danielle standing on the corner of North Avenue and Greenmount, looking down at a body lying on the street. Kashmere runs over, hugs and cries over Rodney's lifeless body.

"What happened? Was it those nigga's we were beefing with last month?"

"No! There was acrossfire between some young street hustlers," Danielle explains. "As Rodney was leaving the corner bar heading for his truck they opened fire."

After the streets were blocked, the media cleared and the spectators disappeared. The police began questioning everybody. They asked Kashmere and Danielle if they saw anything. Kashmere explained he had just arrived and Rodney was his best friend.

On the other hand, Danielle saw the whole thing from the passenger side of Rodney's truck. She also said when they started shooting she ducked down in the truck because she didn't know where those bullets could end up.

She had to give the same statement over and over again. Danielle went back to Rodney's mothers with

Kashmere, trying to explain to him how the whole thing was just a coldblooded murder.

Following the discussion with her, Kashmere directs his full attention to Rodney's mother. Dayshanae calls his cell and starts paging him like crazy, but he didn't want to deal with talking about it at that moment. He turned everything off. All he wanted to do was comfort Rodney's mom.

The next few days were difficult for Rodney's whole family, including Kashmere. He helped with the funeral arrangements. The following Sunday, Kashmere laid his best friend to rest.

Now feeling all alone, Kashmere lounges across his couch watching his usual; *Cartoon Network*. A tear rolls down because he remembers how he and Rodney used to watch it together. His moment of silence is broken by the ringing of the phone.

"Hello?"

"Are you OK?" Dayshanae asks. "Me and mommy just came in."

"Yeah, I'm aiight…just chillin' out. Why what's going on?"

"You should come and stay over here. You just didn't look like yourself at the funeral that's why I hardly said anything to you."

"I feel you, but I'm aiight. I'm just laying low."

"Oh aiight, is it aiight if I come through to check up on you?" she says.

"Yeah, I guess its cool…."

"I guess I'll see you later," Dayshanae informs him as they hang up the phone.

Kashmere sets his answering service to inform folks that call about Rodney's death. This cut the time and conversation of repeating it over and over.

Kashmere was upstairs changing into something comfortable when Dayshanae walked quietly in and took a seat. After five minutes or more she yells upstairs to let him know he has company.

"Hey…boy!"

"How you get in my damn house?" he responds laughing, coming down the stairs. "I know the door was open."

"Oh, I was about to say," she responds reaching out for a hug. Kashmere looked so down.

"Thanks," he responds returning the favor.

Prohibiting Kashmere from doing anything, Dayshanae cooks him a nice meal, since he had refused to eat after the funeral. While he eats, she cleans up a little bit returning the favor from when she was down and out.

Days following, Kashmere stayed camped out alone in the house, rarely talking to anyone other than Dayshanae a few times. Still in his depressed state, Kashmere decides to go out knowing Rodney wouldn't want him cooped up in the house.

On his way out, Sinsation races down the street and runs with open arms towards Kashmere. In the middle of hugging him she cried and squeezed. "I'm soooo sorry! I just heard about Rodney."

"I'm aiight, yo," Kashmere responds trying not to cry.

"Is there anything you need? I mean anything?" she says tighting her grip around him.

"I'll let you know…. I'm just trying to get out the house."

"For real, come on I'll treat you to the movies aiight? Nothing more, nothing less," Sinsation says looking in his eyes with still a good hold on him.

"That sounds good, but maybe another time…. I'm not in the mood for company."

Giving him an off the wall look, but understanding his feelings, she let him loose and walked to her car.

"Just call me, aiight, 'cause when I call you, you won't pick up… Aiight?"

"Aiight, I apologize yo, I'm just not in the mood," He explains to her after seeing the expression on her face.

"Bye Kashmere."

"Bye shorty."

Refusing to go to a club or movies, Kashmere drives out to Hanlon Park and sits on the hood of his car looking at the stars, drinking a fifth of Hennessy.

"Why you, yo, why? Damn, we had the time of our lives in DC and then this bullshit happens. Damn, now I got to struggle this struggle all alone. But I know you still here, looking over me and everybody else. Your mom's in good hands, too. I'll die before something happens to her. But you know I need you, cuzin. But I got to survive…. I miss you, cuzin," he speaks out loud.

Chapter thirteen

With Rodney gone Kashmere tends to keep to himself. From clubs to strip joints he is found to be by himself. Finally, he finds that there is no more fun in his heart in these places without Rodney, so he stops all visits to their old hangouts.

With Danna and Dejah continuing to call, Kashmere sits and explains what happened to Rodney and advises them both to stop calling for him. But the person most hurt out of the whole incident, other than Kashmere is Nyia, since she was the last female Rodney was with physically. He used to keep in touch with her and Jyia especially. After hearing the Rodney situation from Dejah and the twins, Shavon instantly calls Kashmere.

"Hello?" Kashmere answers in a soft voice.

"Hey boy, I just heard what happened to Rodney…. Are you OK?" Shavon questions, the hurt evident in her voice. "This is Shavon."

"Yeah I'm aiight…. Look I might come down there, but I don't know when for sure."

"You know it's whateva, just let me know, but I see you not in the mood to talk so just call me later," she replies waiting for a response.

"Aiight…. I'll do that, I promise," Kashmere says as he hangs up the phone.

Returning to lounge across his bed, he rolls over and falls asleep.

The following day, before he is fully awake there is a knock on the door. Not really being focused, he ignores the knocking. Then the phone begins to ring.

"Hello?"

"You asleep?" Dayshanae questions.

"Who is this?"

"Dayshanae, boy, wake up and come answer the door, then you can go right back to sleep"

"Aiight, here I come."

Kashmere hangs up the phone, sits up and wipes his eyes. Not really paying attention to the phone conversation he just had, he sits for another ten minutes just focusing on himself. Then he lies back down, forgetting that Dayshanae is waiting. Another ten minutes passes and the phone rings again.

"Hello?"

"Boy, get up and come to the door!" Dayshanae yells.

"Huh, who is this…?" he asks falling back asleep.

"Dayshanae. I just called you and told you to open the door."

"Oh shit, I thought I was dreaming. Here I come for real this time."

"For real, boy, come on!" she yells hanging up.

Kashmere jumps to his feet and dashes downstairs. When he opens the door, Dayshanae is standing there with her arms crossed looking furious as hell.

Once inside she bangs him in his chest. "That's for leaving outside all that time."

"You lucky I like your punk-ass, 'cause I would of knocked you out," he replies laughing.

"Whateva, I would beat your ass, too. How you feeling?" she laughs giving him a hug.

"Naw don't hug me now…. You talking shit," He says laughing hugging her back. "So what's going on?"

"Nothing, just being there for you like you were there for me."

"Oh aiight, so you going to cook or was that a one time thing?" he asks with a baby face.

"I'll cook. It just depends what you want and stop looking at me like that, too."

"It don't matter, whateva you want to cook you know I'm not picky. You know what I like," he says going upstairs. "I'll be in the shower."

"Aiight, go wash your funky ass."

"Whateva."

During Kashmere's shower, Dayshanae defrosts some ground turkey to make spaghetti. While it defrosts, she watches *The Cosby Show*, laying across the love seat.

By the end of his shower, the noodles are boiling with the meat cooking beside them. Dayshanae is making herself at home. When he returns downstairs she runs upstairs and snatches a pair of Kashmere's boxers and a wife beater, knowing he would love to see a woman in a wife beater and timberlands. She throws back on her tim's hoping he will give into the temptation.

Back downstairs she walks by, sliding her butt across his woman slayer.

"See, why you wanna start shit? You know you look cute in my shit," he says looking her up and down.

"Thank you.... Now move so I can finish cooking. Go watch TV or something."

"Yes, mother," he responds laughing, walking away.

"Don't start."

"You would know if I was starting something.... Trust me!" Kashmere yells back into the kitchen.

With all the delightful aromas, Kashmere enjoys every smell as he dozes off on the couch.

He is then awakened by Dayshanae, with a tray of spagheti, mixed vegetables and buttered rolls along with a tall glass of ice cold kool-aid. After she sets his tray down, she returns to the kitchen to grab herself a bite to eat.

During their meal they continue to talk shit back and forth, throwing sexual slurs at one another.

"You do, too, you the one I got it from…." She responds laughing, finishing up her meal.

"Whateva, girl."

"Whateva."

"Are you washing dishes or do I have to do them?" Kashmere questions Dayshanae who's standing in the doorway leading him to the kitchen.

"I'll wash them; come in here and relax," she responds pointing to the couch.

Kashmere returns to lounging across the couch, watching the Cartoon Network. When Dayshanae finishes the dishes, she enters the living room and sits in front of Kashmere rubbing his head.

"I know it hurts, but it's going to be OK. I promise you, it does get better," she whispers trying her best to console him.

"I feel you, but I'm trying and the shit hurts."

"I know, and just know I am right here whenever you need me."

"Thanks," Kashmere says wrapping his arms around her waist.

"No problem," she replies lying beside him.

After about four hours, they are still lying across the couch when Kashmere calls Rodney's mom to check up on things.

"Hello?" she answers.

"Hey, mommy, how's everything?"

"As well as to be expected, just taking it day by day! But look, I'm cooking so I'll call you back," she says hanging up the phone.

"OK."

Hearing who Kashmere was talking to, Dayshanae questions, "How is she doing?"

"She's aiight. She's cooking so she said she would call me back."

"Oh, as long as she's OK," Dayshanae replies sitting up. "Hey I'm going to run home, I'll be back."

"Aiight, call my cell, 'cause I might step out."

"OK, I will," she answers giving him a gentle hug.

After she leaves, Kashmere lies down again for ten minutes, then decides to go to the movies alone to see *The Queen of the Damned* Aaliyah's last movie. Right in the middle of the movie, his phone began to vibrate.

"Hello?" he whispers, trying not to disturb anyone from enjoying the movie.

"Hey, where are you?" Dayshanae asks.

"I'm watching *Queen of the Damned,* I'll call you back."

"Aiight, I want to be with you tonight, too. So make sure you call me, OK?"

"You got that…as soon as it's over…. Bye."

"Bye."

The moment the movie is over Kashmere returns Dayshanae's phone call. Before he talks to her, he speaks to her mom and grandmother for at least thirty minutes before Dayshanae realizes he's on the phone. Instead of giving her the phone, they talk for another ten minutes being smart then they allow Dayshanae on the phone.

"You having fun, 'cause I know you were telling them not to give the phone to me," Dayshanae says in a brief slur.

"No I wasn't," he responds laughing.

"Whateva, boy…. Anyways, how was your movie? You sound better too."

"Oh, it was off the hook. You should go see it," Kashmere suggests to her.

"I probably will, I was going to ask your stank butt to take me but I guess that's out the question, huh?" she reponds smartly.

"Shit, I'll go. I told you it was off the hook…matter a fact call and find out what time the last one plays tonight."

"Whateva, stop playin'."

"Do it sound like I'm playing? Call and find out. I'll be there in ten minutes. Bye," Kashmere says hanging up and racing straight to her house.

When he arrives, Dayshanae doesn't allow him inside knowing her mother and grandmother would talk him to death. She runs out to his car.

"Here are all the times," she says handing him a piece of paper. While he looks it over, she sits quietly listening to some slow jam CD Kashmere had made a while ago. Deciding to go to the movies the following day, they go back in the house and lie quietly across Dayshanae's bed. She slowly glides her fingers across Kashmere's head causing him to dose off to sleep.

Chapter fourteen

If losing Rodney wasn't enough pain on Kashmere and Dayshanae they would soon find more. They sat along with her mother and cried dearly over the silent death of grandma. At least she wasn't in any pain or illness she just drifted off to the Lord in her sleep. While the preacher prayed over her soul, Kashmere consoled Dayshanae like she consoled him when Rodney died.

"Hey calm down…. I know it's hard, but like everybody told me she's in a better place, happy and with no pain."

"I know, but I miss her already, she was one of my best friends other than mom and you," Dayshanae cried while the tears just rolled down her cheeks.

After trying to calm her down, they returned home where dinner was being served. Refusing to eat, Dayshanae kept to herself in her room. Not taking 'no' for an answer, Kashmere prepares her plate along with his and proceeds to Dayshanae's room.

"Here, I know you don't want to eat, but you need to…or whenever you're ready, the food is right here," Kashmere says placing her plate down on the nightstand beside her.

"Oh! And don't think you're leaving this room until you've finished eating something. Matter a fact wait until I finish eating."

"Why are you acting like that?" she asks wiping her tears.

"Like what? Your ass needs to eat."

"Look I'll eat damn, then will you stop bothering me?"

"I'm not bothering you yet.... I was going to feed your ass if you wanted to eat or not, that's why I said wait."

"Look I'm eating, seeeee?" she replies grabbing the fork on the plate and beginning to eat. Making sure her plate is cleaned to the last crumb, Kashmere returns to the kitchen to rinse their plates off and place them inside the dishwasher.

Before he goes back upstairs, he kisses and hugs Ms. Brenda to let her know everything will be OK.

Dayshanae is lying across her bed trying to watch *Baby Boy,* but she can't concentrate, all she can think of is grandma.

"Boy, Tyreece reminds me of you in this movie," she explains as Kashmere enters the room.

"Man, whateva.... How you figure?"

"'Cause you a big mama's boy and you don't have no baby-momma's but you got mad females."

"Whateva.... I'm not trying to hear that bullshit," Kashmere responds lying behind her.

"You know it's true that's why you not trying to hear it."

"Yeah, aiight girl, watch the movie," he responds once again ignoring her every word.

"Yeah, OK," Dayshanae says returning her focus back to the movie.

Checking on his niece, one of her uncles shouts upstairs. Replying that everything's OK, she satisfies his question and he returns to his business controlling downstairs.

At the end of the movie, Dayshanae turns to Kashmere and attempts to talk to him about his feelings toward comittment or relationships in general, not just with her but with anyone.

"So, Mr. Kashmere, why are you really single? Are you scared of comittment or just want to play the field?"

"Damn where's that coming from? Why everytime we watch a movie you always come to me with mad questions?" Kashmere asks. "But to answer your question, I haven't found the right one for me and frankly I'm not looking. No, I am not scared, like I just said I'm not looking."

"OK, I hear that but what about the playing the field?" she says sitting halfway up.

"I'm playing the field for right now, but I'm about to let all that shit go real soon."

"Why?"

"Cause I'm getting real tired of the bullshit out there, the games and everything that goes along with the playing. I'm getting too old for that shit," Kashmere replies fixing some of her pillows behind him.

"So when you plan on stopping?"

"I don't know, but it's going to be real soon… I'm about to go home, you aiight?"

"Yeah, I'm aiight just call me. I'm going to sleep" she responds hugging him. "Thank you."

"No problem, shorty," Kashmere responds returning the hug and walking out the door.

On his way out, he tells everyone goodnight and heads for his place. When he arrives home, Kashmere finds two messages from Shavon, checking on how he was doing. After settling in, he returns her call.

"Hey, shorty…" Kashmere says when she answers with a "Hello?"

"How are you doing Mr. Man? Are you OK?"

"Yeah, I'm aiight I guess, but my friend Dayshanae just buried her grandmother earlier today and she was like my grandmother, too, so I'm also feeling very bad."

"Damn, sorry to hear that. First Rodney, and then her, are you sure you're OK?" she asks again showing her concern.

"Yeah I should be, but good looking out."

"You know I'm always looking out for you boy," Shavon says, "I might try to come see you in a month or two OK?"

"That's cool, just let me know when…" Kashmere replies diving across his bed. "But I'll call you later, I'm about to go to sleep for like an hour or two."

"Aiight, boy."

The second he hangs up the phone he quickly drifts off to sleep.

The following day, Kashmere feels a little stressed and it was only one person that understood him really…it was Rodney. With him being gone, Kashmere drives out to the gravesite, kneels down, and just talks about his feelings, like Rodney was never gone. Hour after hour the words flow out making Kashmere feel a whole lot better. Before leaving he lays a long stem rose across the site and whispers,

"Damn, Cuzin, I wish it was me that was gone… I know you're still with me in spirit, and I know you're always looking out for me like my guardian angel… Man, I miss you and love you cuzin."

On his way home, Dayshanae called looking for him.

"Where you at boy?" She asked.

"Leaving Rodney's site… I needed to talk with him."

"Oh are you OK?"

"Yeah, I feel a lot better. So what's going on?" He replies, stopping at a red light.

"Nothing. Are you in the mood for company, 'cause I really need to be around somebody… I feel alone without my grandmother here," Dayshanae asks. Kashmere could hear the pain in her voice.

"You know when you need me I'm there, so I'm on my way," he explains as he races towards her house.

At his arrival, Dayshanae spots him parking as she looks out her window. She hops up and rushes downstairs where she meets him at the door.

"What's up…?" He greets her.

"Nothing now. You're here and that's what I wanted, you here with me. 'Cause I feel you are all I have, other than my mother," she says smiling and crying at the same time.

"Damn, I didn't know you felt like that."

"Well, it's a lot of things you don't know," Dayshanae responds hugging him tightly.

"Well, tell me then."

"I will, but just hold me for a while."

"OK" Kashmere said enjoying the embrace of her touch.

Chapter fifteen

The following week, Dayshanae explains all her feelings to Kashmere, from middle school to the present. How her love has grown day by day; year by year, while they lie close caressing each other softly and slowly building up an inner heat.

"Your fingertips feel so good," Dayshanae whispers while she kisses upon his neck.

"Ummm why you starting?" Kashmere asks enjoying the touch of her lips.

"Starting what? I'm not doing anything."

"Naw, you ain't doing nothing just starting shit that you know you can't finish."

"I can finish it, trust me. Let me show you," Dayshanae starting to inch her way down Kashmere's neck. With delicate fingertips she cruises down his back then she reaches the beginning of his waistline, sending electric sexual pulses up his spine. While temptation helps urge her on more, Kashmere relaxes during the plunging of his pole which boxes with the tonsils in every upward and downward motion of Dayshanae's head.

"Damn…." Kashmere silently releases in a whisper.

Feeling left out of the pleasure, Dayshanae turns and places the splits of paradise, dripping wet, upon his glazed soft lips. Deep into the moment with the touch of a few flips, Dayshanae is found straddled on top of him displaying her other hidden talents.

In the air nothing is heard but soft moans and purified splashs of moisture upon skin. With every bounce, walls receive knocks causing Dayshanae to calm down the roughness to a calm stroke. Switching positions with a gentle touch, Kashmere places her on her back and suddenly eases himself back inside her tomb of unbelievable fulfillment.

After each thrust, Dayshanae's mind starts to boggle as orgasmic tention builds. With Kashmere knocking at the door she finally opens up to release waterfalls of overpowering forces from within. Her body shakes then suddenly freezes. Her eyes disappear behind darkness as they travel backwards.

After it is all finished, insides have been demolished, new frontiers explored and long lost treasures released. Dayshanae's eyes return to the light, pulling her from the dreamland of ectasy back to reality where Kashmere lays quietly with a gentle grasp on her body. The following ten minutes are bumpy as aftershocks of vibrating pulses surge through her body, releasing streams of dwelling moisture that missed the grand opening minutes ago.

"Damn, it's like that…?" Kashmere questions.

"What…? What are you talking about?" she responds stuttering as the shocks continued.

"Nothing… I'm going to take a shower, you can join me if you want."

"That's aiight… you go ahead. I can't move right now and you dangerous. I got to watch out for you," Dayshanae says pulling the sheets up to her neck.

"Is that a good or bad thing?" Kashmere asks.

Dayshanae just looks at him with an unspeakable smile on her face.

Kashmere shows her a little smirk then closes the door behind him as he heads for the shower.

Just when Kashmere is finishing his shower Dayshanae walks in.

"Don't turn off the shower."

"Oh, aiight…" he responds stepping out as she steps in.

Now fully dry, Kashmere looks himself over in the mirror noticing he needs a haircut to bring back the nice smooth bald head.

"I need a haircut."

"What hair are you going to cut?" Dayshanae questions scarcastically. "I'll cut it for you."

"Oh, hell no you won't."

"Why not…? You don't trust me?"

"I won't even let my own mother cut my hair and she brought me into the world. You might get a flashback or something and cut me all up," Kashmere starts laughing.

"Whatever, boy."

As Dayshanae continues to shower, Kashmere leaves to get dressed and make an appointment with his barber. He wants his barber to meet him at his house. Kashmere informs Dayshanae that he'll be back and heads out the door.

Returning home, he places a chair in the middle of the basement floor to prepare where he's going to receive the haircut. Twenty-minutes later, his friend Kenny arrived.

Lounging in the chair as the clippers glide across his head, Kashmere and Kenny talk about all the crazy shit they both went through with females. After Kenny told his war stories Kashmere quickly interrupts.

"I don't care what you say, this bitch I was screwing with, name Sinsation, was crazy as shit. She was one of the 'Fatal attraction' situations. She came over this way cutting motherfucka's…" he stops Kenny from cutting his hair to show his battle scar.

"Damn, shorty, what you fuck! Yeah, you right none of my broads are that crazy."

While Kenny puts the finishing touches on his work the phone starts to ring.

"Yo, pass me the phone please," Kashmere asks as Kenny hands him the phone.

"Hello?"

"Hey how are you doing?" the familiar voice says.

"Who dis?"

"This is Danna, Stacey's friend."

"Oh, what's going on?" Kashmere responds noticing who he's talking to finally.

"Nothing, I was just calling to see if you were aiight, 'cause I know it's hard without Rodney."

"Yeah, I'm cool. When I need to talk to him, I just go see him."

"I feel that. Hey, me and Stacey fell off on the friendship, but you were always cool to me, so I called you…and I wanted to ask you something also," she explains.

"What's up?"

"I'll be in Baltimore later tonight and I was wondering if I could stop by?"

"That's aiight with me, just call to make sure I'm here."

"OK, I'll do that… Talk to you then," she responds as they hang up.

"Bye…"

"Bye, shorty."

By the time he finally got off the phone, Kenny had finished and walked out the door. Running upstairs after he cleaned up all the scattered hair from the floor, Kashmere enters the bathroom to wash off the excess hair from his freshly smooth head. Following the washing of his head he calls Dayshanae and explains to her that he would be there a little later than he thought because he was expecting company.

"Who's coming over there?"

"Rodney's old shorty from DC," he responds.

"Who the freak ya'll always visited in DC?" Dayshanae questioned. "If it's her, that broad trying to screw you since Rodney, her best friend is gone."

"We don't roll like that and she got mad feelings for Rodney, even more now that he's gone," he debated towards her statement.

"Just watch.... That's all I'm saying is watch. Call me when she leaves and you better not screw her or it's going to be some De'Ja Vu cutting serious."

"Girl whatever, I'll call you back," he says hanging up the phone not allowing her to say another word.

He then started preparing for Danna's arrival.

Chapter sixteen

Finally the call he'd been waiting for came. Remembering the number from the first time Danna called, Kashmere refused to say "Hello."

"Where you at?"

"On Hartford Rd and North Avenue" she answered.

Within ten minutes Kashmere had directed her to his house and they were face to face once again after a couple of months without any contact. Just one look into Kashmere's eyes Danna burst into tears 'cause she could see and feel the pain he was trying to hide.

Holding him close Danna continued to cry which caused Kashmere to cry by chain reaction.

"You know you're hurting and I don't understand why you're trying to hold it in… That's not good for you at all." Danna blurts out.

"I know, but I hate showing everybody how I feel 'cause they take advantage of you when you're weak."

"That's true, but you still could tell somebody you trust." She adds.

"I do. That's when I'm talking to Rodney."

"Oh, is that the only person you trust or trusted?" Danna inquires.

"No, but that's the only person that really understood me to the fullest."

"I feel you, not trying to say I'm not interested but we need to brighten the night up. I missed seeing your crazy ass."

"Whateva, you ain't even paid me any damn mind. Your whole attention was on Rodney," Kashmere sits down laughing.

"He was dicking me down so I had to pay attention to him."

"I feel you. I'm not hating; I loved it. At least someone was showing him some love."

"But now he's gone and I got to search for someone else to focus my attention on," Danna discretely whispers under her breath with a disceitful smile.

"Well, where are you looking?"

"I haven't made my mind up yet, still searching," she says rubbing along his leg.

"So, I figure you searching over this way now, huh?"

"Only if you willing to allow me to search," Danna responds, moving her hand to his inner thigh.

"Yo, I think you need to reroute 'cause I got too much respect for my boy," Kashmere says grabbing her hand.

"It's not like me and him were together, we just fucked. So you wouldn't be disrespecting nobody."

"I feel what you saying, but that's my boy…and I would feel better if he was still here, but you know"

"So, you going to turn me down?" Danna replies as she stands up removing her shirt and jeans revealing how luscious and plump her breasts and ass are.

"Damn, I mean…," He says biting his bottom lip.

Looking him up and down she begins to slowly move her body, giving him a little strip show made just for him. Not wanting to spoil the moment she turns on R. Kelly's song 'Naked' from the Rest of Both Worlds CD.

To every beat her body moves as her thongs inch down showing her perfectly shaved soaking wet universe of satisfaction.

Enticing him more, Danna lifts his shirt and gently she gazes in his eyes waiting for access to his unauthorized area.

Caught up in the moment, Kashmere gives a slight nod, as she unbuckles his pants and begins her search. Right before she can fully grab the now extended rod, Kashmere flashes back to reality and stops all cause of her search.

"Yo…Yo! Stop, I can't do this shit!" Kashmere says grabbing her hands.

"Why can't you?" she questions trying to wrap her tongue around his manhood. Noticing what she's attempting to do Kashmere jumps back gently leaving Danna in suspense, knowing now she's getting turned down.

"So you really stopping me?" Danna asks.

"Yeah, I ain't playing, truthfully. I think you need to be going," Kashmere responds fully standing up on his feet. "So come on," he adds, helping her to her feet and tossing her clothes right behind her.

"That's messed up."

"No, what's messed up is you screwed my boy, then he dies and your trying now to screw his closest friend, you might as well say family," Kashmere expresses in an uproar.

"Look, I wanted both of ya'll when we first met and I figured I could have both, but I guess I can't huh?" Danna asks now in a full attire.

"I guess not," Kashmere responds opening the door. With hurt feelings along with a broke down face, Danna walks out the door.

When she is totally out, she decides to try to say another statement, but when she turns to Kashmere he slams the door and proceeds to answer ringing phone. He leaves all thoughts of Danna on the opposite side on the door.

"Hello?"

"Hi, Kashmere," the sweet mature voice greets him.

"Hey, ma… How you holding up?" He asks Rodney's mom.

"I'm as well as to be expected, I was calling you to tell you some good news."

"What's going on?"

"You know Mr. Johnson was a big time business man here in Baltimore, and when he passed away he left me and Rodney all his assets," she calmly explains. "I just spoke with the lawyer and Rodney has left you one million dollars. He felt you were like the brother he never had," she added.

Being shocked, with tears rolling down his face Kashmere sits quietly, surprised by what she just said.

"Kashmere… Kashmere? Are you there?" she calls out.

"Yeah, I'm here."

"Baby, it's OK. Come to my house tomorrow and I'll give you the check."

"OK ma, thank you. I just can't believe it," he answers.

"No, thank you for being there for Rodney," she responds crying. "I'll see you tomorrow."

"OK," he says hanging the phone up very gently. "Is this a dream or did she really say what I think she said," Kashmere thinks out loud.

Not worrying about the time, Kashmere dashes out to Rodney's site. At his arrival he notices flowers and pictures all over his grave. Pictures of Rodney and his mother and of him. As he sits down and becomes comfortable, Kashmere begins to talk to his lost friend.

"What's up, cuzin? I see mom's stopped by. But I'm here to truly thank you. You always told me that you'd always be here and if you had it, I had it. Yo! You shocked the shit out of me with them bills cuzin. I only wish we were together to spread the wealth."

Stopping all his conversation, Kashmere begins to pray asking for the spoken word of God, and for Rodney to lead him in the right direction. After a few minutes, he returns home and continues to relax. Before he can get fully comfortable his phone begins to ring.

"Hello?"

"What you doing boy?" Dayshanae questions.

"Chillin', can you come over?" says Kashmere.

"Yeah, I'll be over in like five minutes," she responds.

"Aiight."

While he waits for her arrival, Kashmere takes out a pack of steaks to defrost. As soon as Dayshanae walks in, Kashmere hits her with the good news.

"For real, a million dollars?" she shouts.

"Shhh, damn you, trying to get a nigga robbed or something?" he responds calming her down.

"Oh, my bad."

"Now sit down and chill out, while I go season this food," Kashmere suggests handing her the remote.

"What you cooking? How can you be so calm about a million dollars?" she asks not knowing Kashmere is in the kitchen dancing and jumping around. Then with a calm voice he answers her question.

"Steak, and I got to find something to fix with it."

"Try some greens, corn or something with some potatoes. So you gonna quit your job?" asks Dayshanae.

"I don't know what I'm gonna do. Aiight? So, will you calm your hyper ass down?" Kashmere replies returning to the kitchen.

While he prepares the food, he notices Dayshanae is too quiet.

"Hey… Hey Dayshanae," he calls out.

When he walks in the living room she's stretched out across the couch asleep. Leaving her in peace, Kashmere turns off the TV and covers her with a sheet, then returns to his meal.

Chapter seventeen

It's been four days since Kashmere deposited the check and he hasn't spent a dime on anything but bills. He is still in shock. To stop all the stress of his monthly payments he just cleared his whole credit report paying everything off, making him debt free and the owner of everything in his possession.

Not being real flashy with jewelry, he decids to change his wardrobe and gives Dayshanae a couple of thousand dollars to help her and her mom out. Then he has thoughts of buying himelf a house or condo.

"Boy, I can't take your money… Rodney left this for you," Dayshanae says.

"OK, and it's mine right? So now it's yours…just take it," Kashmere responds placing the money in her hand.

"See, that's why me and my mother love your crazy ass so much. 'Cause you can be as sweet as hell when you want to be," she says hugging him tightly.

"OK, thank you," he whispers gasping for air.

"Oh, I'm sorry I'm just happy."

"I wish you were my man. I mean I'm glad you're my friend," she slips up and says.

Refraining to respond, Kashmere returns the hug and lets her know that he'll be back.

"Aiight, I'll be here. I'll call you if I leave."

"Aiight."

Not really having any particular place to go, Kashmere just drives around thinking about what so-called slipped out of Dayshanae's mouth. Having thought about a relationship with Dayshanae before, it just seems to him that someone or something wants them together. It wasn't enough that her grandmother, her mom or Rodney kept telling him they were going to get married one day. Day after day it seemed like they got closer and closer, but it was always something that got in the way, either a female on his part or a male on hers.

Ending up at the mall, he goes to Zales Jewelry and just looks over all the diamond rings. Knowing he's not ready for a comittment like that, he heads back to Dayshanae's.

Halfway out the door, he hears a familiar voice shouting his name. Turning around he notices Sinsation heading straight in his direction.

"What's up, boy?"

"Ain't shit…what's up with you?"

"Nothing. I was going to call you yesterday, but something came up," she explains.

"Damn sure glad you didn't call I wish you didn't see me now," he mumbles to himself. "But look," he says so she can hear, "I'm running late for this engagement so I'll holla at you later."

"Can I go?" She asks.

"You must really think I'll still screw wit you like that. Hell, no," he responds trying to walk out the door.

Chasing behind him, Sinsation yells out his name. "Kashmere! Kashmere, why you acting like this?" she asks grabbing onto him.

With an angry look on his face he stares down at her hand. Noticing the look on his face she quickly removes her hand.

"Why you acting like that?"

"'Cause I don't have time to put up with your shit," he responds walking away. "So, I'll holla, and I have a woman anyways."

"Who, that bitch Dayshanae, that phoney bitch?"

Ignoring her loud ignorant ass he continues on the path to his car. Still hearing her clearly, he jumps in and pulls off. Racing straight for her, Kashmere nearly runs her over, not caring about the consequences.

Stopping at the light right outside the mall parking lot, he sits patiently listening to RL's Elements CD when all of a sudden something pushes him from behind, jerking his car.

"What the fuck?" he yells out looking in his rear view mirror, seeing Sinsation ramming her car into the back of his Benz.

During her preparation to ram him again, he also prepares himself. As she stepped on the gas, her tires back spinned and just before she could hit him, Kashmere quickly turned into busy traffic. Luckily, keeping her foot on the gas, Sinsation came out unharmed and untouched.

Still worked up, Kashmere calls Dayshanae.

"Hello?" she answers with a laughing tone.

"Hello, what you doing?" he asks. "Nevermind, I hear your loud ass friend. Anyways, yo, me and Sinsation got into it again and she rammed into my car," he adds.

"For real? I told you that bitch is crazy," she says laughing.

"What's so funny?"

"Nothing, boo, I'm drinking some Henne with Mika. Oh, my bad, my loud ass friend," she says still laughing.

"Whateva, well I'll be over there."

"Aiight…see you when you get here."

Allowing Dayshanae time to trip with Mika, it takes Kashmere thirty minutes to get to the house. Being used to just walking in, he heads straight upstairs, noticing no one's home. Kashmere tiptoes upstairs, to try and scare her like he does sometimes.

As he reaches the door, all he hears is the 'Feeling Your Booty' remix by R. Kelly combined with the soft tone of moans. Just ignoring the moans, figuring it was part of the song, Kashmere creeps in. With the door halfway open, he spots a scene that would make any man happy. Frozen in his tracks, he watches as Dayshanae runs her fingers through Mika's hair, while she licks upon Dayshanae's island of love, making Dayshanae quiver and tug her hair.

Not knowing she is being watched, Dayshanae continues to allow her to taste. Mika, on the other hand, notices and gives Kashmere a slight wave to enter along with a smirk of enjoyment. Closing the door tight so there wouldn't be any more interruptions, Kashmere continues to watch as his manhood inches down his leg to its full attention.

Knowing he likes every sight of this, Mika waves for him to come closer. As soon as he is close enough she grabs his hand and places it on Dayshanae's thigh. Feeling a third hand, Dayshanae jumps knowing now that her and Mika are not alone.

"Stop! Stop, Mika," Dayshanae whispers.

"Why?" Mika asks between each slurp of juices.

"'Cause Kashmere is here."

"Girl, let her finish her work of art. I've been here a good while now."

Not really listening Dayshanae falls back into the world of estasy. Kashmere watches on and rubs along Dayshanae's thigh, making her moan even louder.

"Did you lock the door?" Mika asks.

"Yeah."

"Don't worry, my mother went out of town for a couple of days anyway. The door was only open in the first place because I knew he was..." Dayshanae whispers between each moan. "...coming," she finally finishes her statement.

"Aiight, cool..." Mika responds going back to what she was doing.

As he stands there, Mika decides to add him more into the situation. With Kashmere focused on Dayshanae's reactions, Mika surprises him by rubbing along his third extension. Feeling good and tempted, he pays her no mind while she lets his special friend reveal itself to the light.

Making him switch positions with her, he begins to catch the juices flowing from Dayshanae as Mika swallows the long and wide pole of Kashmere whole. Feeling the off the hook skills of Mika, Kashmere can't concentrate on licking the Dayshanae's jewels.

Noticing the two are going at it, Dayshanae sits up and pulls Kashmere onto the bed. After he's comfortably situated on the bed, Dayshanae along with Mika begins to devoir every bit of Kashmere's body.

While Dayshanae kisses below his waist line, Mika joins her after a few licks above. With his tool gulped between the gums of Dayshanae, Kashmere's dangling friends are twirled around by the tongue of Mika.

"Damn…" Kashmere says rubbing his hands through the hair on each of their heads. Minute after minute, they make Kashmere feel like he's sitting on top of the world. Following about twenty minutes Dayshanae jumps aboard the ruler that only a man can carry naturally, and it splashes deep into her ocean of pleasure. With every bounce, it drives deeper and deeper. Dayshanae watches Mika fondle herself, making her body overflow. Not wanting to be selfish, Mika straddles Kashmere's face and allows him to taste a little.

"Oh shit…um, Oh shit" Mika moaned out. "I'm about to cum."

Leaning back as Dayshanae grabs hold of her, Mika releases the candies from within. Kissing upon her lips Dayshanae also releases her treats. After every drop is out, neither of them are nowhere finished. Dayshanae switches positions with Mika not giving Kashmere any insight on the situation. Before Dayshanae takes her seat, Kashmere expresses his feelings.

"So, ya'll just going to take control like that, huh?"

"Yep, now shut up 'cause you know you love it," the drunken Dayshanae says sitting down.

Following the position switch about thirty minutes later, they all experience one of the best orgasms that satisfies them all. Experiencing this, both ladies lay close under Kashmere with arms wrapped tight around him.

"Damn, to be a smart ass, you off the hook…" Mika says, applying the statement towards Kashmere.

"You ain't bad yourself, loud ass," he responds as they both laugh.

In the middle of laughter, they take a look at Dayshanae who has fell fast asleep.

"Her drunk ass is asleep," Kashmere says moving her arms so she can lay comfortable.

During Dayshanae's little nap, Kashmere takes a shower. Before that he locks the door behind Mika as she heads home. After twenty minutes of showering, Kashmere returns to a still fast asleep Dayshanae. While she sleeps, he laughs to himself about what had just happened, still in shock.

Chapter eighteen

The next day Kashmere acts like nothing happened, not saying a word about the situation. He tries his best to stay far away from it totally, until later that night. While he and Dayshanae are eating, she surprises him with a question.

"So, did you like it or what?"

"Huh?" he responds not thinking she remembered the situation.

"You heard me."

"Yeah, I liked it… It was aiight," he says filling his mouth with food.

"OK, I'm glad you enjoyed it, 'cause it was a once in a lifetime thing," she says. "But anyways, what were you saying yesterday about Sinsation?" she adds, changing the subject instantly.

Kashmere can't believe she remembers everything he told her about the whole mall incident. After hearing the rest of the drama Dayshanae sits quiet for two minutes then calmly says.

"Fuck that crazy bitch! If I knew you fucking with her I would of warned you of her crazy ass."

"I'm not worried about it, but why you changing the subject? Why that can't happen again? I'm not saying I want it again; I'm just curious why it's a one-time thing?"

"Whateva, nigga, you know if you could do it every day you would."

"Hey, that's different, ya'll would be offering. I'm no gay nigga. I'm not going to turn ya'll down," he says laughing.

"Whateva, just get it out your head 'cause it ain't happening no more!"

"Damn, OK, I was just asking."

"Don't ask no more…" Dayshanae says laughing.

"I said aiight…" he says lying across her bed.

While she finishes off her food, Kashmere flips through the TV, from channel to channel.

"Can you please pick one channel?" Dayshanae asks in a playful mood.

"Look, you focus on that plate and stop worrying about what I'm doing."

As he turned back to watch TV, she set down her plate and slapped him upside his head with a pillow.

"I'm going to let you slide…next time I'm just going to bust that ass," Kashmere says smiling.

"Whateva, nigga. You ain't going to do shit," Dayshanae responds swinging the pillow.

Just before the pillow connects to his head, he pops up and grabs it. Snatching the pillow from her, he turns the table of the pillow fight. After every hit, Kashmere talks to her like a parent beating a child.

"Didn't I tell you…not to hit me?"

"You still ain't shit," she continues to say laughing, receiving every blow. "Kashmere…stop. I feel sick…hold up."

Hearing this, he quickly hops off the bed just in time to be missed by the vomit flow that now covers the whole bed.

"Oh shit…I'm sorry. I'm so sorry," she says wiping her mouth.

"Damn, I'll be back...you aiight, though?"

"Yeah..."

Kashmere rushes out the door to retrieve something to clean up the mess. When he returns, Dayshanae has opened all her windows and wrapped all her sheets in a bundle.

"Just get a trash bag."

"Oh, aiight," he responds turning back around. "You non-drinking punk!" he shouts running down the stairs laughing.

"Forget you!" she yells back.

Finally finishing up, Kashmere decides to take Dayshanae outside for some fresh air. Still laughing and joking, Kashmere continues to pick with her.

"You lucky I didn't do it on you..."

"No, you lucky you didn't do it on me. I would of whooped that ass..." Kashmere says as his phone begins to ring.

"Hello?" Jiya asks with her sister and Shavon laughing in the background.

"Who is this?" he asks, not recoginizing the voice.

"Hey, Shavon's acting like you don't know her now. Here take the phone," she responds handing Shavon the phone.

Kashmere laughs, now knowing who it is.

"You don't know nobody..." Shavon says.

"Yeah...but ya'll crazy. Motherfuckers don't call me. What's going on, shorty?"

"Nothing, chillin'... What's going on with you, you big pimp," she says laughing.

"Pimp? I ain't no pimp!" he shouts.

When Dayshanae hears that she begins to yell in the background.

"Whateva, boy, you got mad girls. You in front of one right now. See! See, who is that you pimping?"

"Whateva, that my homegirl, Dayshanae."

"Let me talk to her…" Shavon suggests.

"For what?"

"Just put her on the phone."

"Man, whateva… Here, girl, telephone," he says handing Dayshanae the phone.

With Dayshanae on the phone with Shavon, Kashmere sits down and listens carefully to their every word, assuring nothing but the ordinary is talked about. He gives them five minutes to talk.

Kashmere grabs for the phone. "Aiight, time's up!"

"Whateva, boy, you better go ahead…" Dayshanae responds pushing his hand away.

"Girl, stop playing. Give me the phone."

Repaying him for all his jokes and game playing, Dayshanae runs away dodging his every attempt to get the phone.

"You wanted to joke with me about throwing up, right? Holla at you shorty," she says laughing and races for the front door.

Cutting her plans short, Kashmere beats her to the door and regains his phone.

"Oh, ya'll want to play?" he says referring to both Dayshanae and Shavon.

"No, calm down boy… But I'll call you later on this week aiight?" Shavon responds hanging up.

"So you want to play right?"

"Naw…see what happens…" she says laughing.

"See what happens, my ass," he says as she dashes off the porch knowing she was in for it.

After chasing her around, Kashmere finally grabs her and carefully tickles her, trying his best not to make her hurl again. Kashmere does it for only a few seconds.

Right after their playing time, Kashmere heads home. The minute he walks in the door, his phone rings.

"Damn, can I get in the house?" he thinks out loud to himself, just before answering the phone.

"Hello?"

"How you doing?" the person asks.

"Who is this?"

"This is Danna…"

"Ya, I told you before I don't fuck with you…so holla," he responds by hanging up, cutting anything that would be said by her short.

Being kind of tired, he heads for his bed. Before going to bed, he plans to just sleep for an hour or two but he ends up sleeping the night away.

The following day Kashmere wakes up to an overflow of calls on the Caller ID. Dayshanae called, Shavon called and even Sinsation. Paying no mind to calls from Sinsation, he returns the calls from Dayshanae first being short and quick.

"What's up, shorty?" he says as she picks up the phone.

"What happened to you last night?"

"I fell asleep, but I'll be over in like an hour, aiight?"

"Aiight…go brush your teeth 'cause you sound like you breath stinks," she says laughing.

"Well I guess breath is through… 'cause you sound like your phone is screaming damn," he replies quickly saying the first thing coming to his head.

"Boy, whateva…just hurry up."

"Aiight, I'll be there," he says hanging up.

Not really in a rush to return Shavon's call, he jumps in the shower and lounges around grabbing a bite to eat before he finally calls her. When he does call her, he gets no answer.

Right before Kashmere walks out the door to Dayshanae's he hears a car pealing down the street. Paying no attention 'cause that is like an everyday thing around where he lives, but when he reaches his car he notices his tires are slashed and a note is posted on the windshield. Knowing who would have done this, he snatches the note, not even reading it and runs in the house to call Dayshanae to come get him.

When she picks up, he gives her no chance to say hello.

"Yo, come get me…"

"What's wrong?" she asks noticing the tone in his voice.

"Yo, I'll tell you when you get here."

"Aiight, I'm on my way."

"Aiight."

As he waits, he reads the note left by Sinsation, which reads:

Hey Bitch,

You wanted to screw me, but still decided to go to that bitch. i call and you don't return my calls, so since i'm not trying to go to jail for killing or just fucking you up for life. i decided to fuck up the closet thing to you. This pretty ass Benz... Don't return my calls again and see what happens.

That Bitch Sinsation.

Frustrated about the letter, but pissed off because of his car. Kashmere sits out on the front steps waiting for Dayshanae who arrives three minutes later. Racing up to the porch in a pair of sweats and a white tee, Dayshanae approaches Kashmere.

"What's happening?" Not saying a word, Kashmere hands her the note.

"What's this and what the fuck happened to your car?"

"Just read the note," he says leaning back on the stairs.

Reading every word, she starts to take it to heart.

"I told you to stop screwing with that bitch."

"I did… The bitch is crazy. She was your girl first, remember?" he says being sarcastic.

"So what, but you the one that screwed her and knowing you…you probably screwed her as good as you screwed me."

"Whateva, I just need to get my baby fixed," Kashmere responds referring to his car.

"Aren't you gonna call the police."

"What for, what they gonna do?"

"Ok we will…let me call my peoples, where's your phone?"

Having the phone right next to him, he quickly hands it to her.

"How much is it going to cost?" He questions.

"It's going to be cheap, it's my cousin…Darrel," she answers when Darrel finally picks up the phone.

Explaining the situation and giving him directions to Kashmere's house, Dayshanae hangs up and waits for Darrel to arrive along with Kashmere. Twenty-five minutes later, a black Ford pick-up pulls up with four brand new tires in the back.

As Darrel unloads his truck, Kashmere goes down to introduce himself.

"What's up man?"

"Nothing. Darrel, yo."

"Kashmere."

"So you're the famous Kashmere that my cousin's crazy about," Darrel says.

"Oh really, she crazy about me?"

Before Darrel could let out all of Dayshanae's secrets she comes down to the car. "Shut up Darrel, you talk too much," she says pushing his shoulder.

"Naw, Darrel, go ahead," Kashmere laughs.

"Naw. Yo, you on your own with that, she crazy. I should know…she's family," Darrel says as he begins to change the busted tires.

"Don't worry about what he got to say, just worry about your car, punk."

"Look Ms. Hurl O' mighty stay out of grown folks bizness," Kashmere responds laughing, looking at the fine job Darrel is doing.

Fifteen minutes later, Kashmere is thanking Darrel.

"So how much do I owe you?"

"Don't worry about it. This one's on me, just take care of my cuzin."

"Thanks and no problem. I'll always do that. She's my little shorty."

"Aiight," Darrel says laughing. "Here's my card if you have any problems or whateva."

"Aiight, goodlooking."

They show each other love and Darrel goes his separate way, leaving Kashmere and Dayshanae behind.

"You lucky I like your bald head," says Dayshanae watching while Kashmere locks the rims onto his new tires.

"Whateva, you lucky I like you punk ass."

"Whateva, boy. Whenever you finish playing with your baby come down my house," she says running her nails across his head.

"Aiight, I shouldn't be long."

"You better not be," she says opening her car door.

"See there you go… always talking shit."

"Boy, whateva…" Dayshanae replies sitting down.

Just before she closes the door, Kashmere yells out her name.

"Dayshanae! Hey Dayshanae!"

"What, boy?" she says standing up.

"Thanks."

"You welcome, just hurry up and bring your pretty boy ass to my house," she responds shutting the door in a hurry, knowing she was about to hear it for calling him pretty boy.

Giving her a slight frown as she pulls off, Kashmere continues to lock his rims completely to the car. Showering right afterwards, being covered in dirt and oil, he quickly throws on a sweatsuit and heads for Dayshanae's.

Ka'Shus

Chapter nineteen

When Ms. Brenda arrives home, she's welcomed by a home cooked meal prepared by Kashmere just for her.

"Thank you, baby."

"Just put those bags down and take a seat. Dayshanae will put your stuff up and I'll make your plate."

"OK, what ya'll two up to?" Ms. Brenda asks.

"Nothing, why can't me and your daughter just cook you dinner?"

"Ya'll can, but I know both of ya'll too well."

"OK, I know, but it's always a first for everything," Kashmere laughs placing the plate in front of her while grabbing the second bag that Dayshanae left behind.

Carefully putting her clothes in their proper places, Dayshanae and Kashmere make her return home peaceful and easy as ever. Ms. Brenda finishes her dinner, takes a shower and heads for bed thanking them both for everything.

Sitting and watching TV as Kashmere washes the dishes, Dayshanae hears Kashmere's cell phone ringing in the other room so she goes to retrieve it for him.

"Hello?"

"Hey, how are you holding up? Shavon told me she talked to you," Jiya said.

"I'm doing aiight. Chillin' with my shorty."

"Who? Dayshanae, yeah I heard about her."

"What you hear?" he questions curiously.

"Nothing bad… I just called to ask a question."

"What's up?"

"So, you settling down or can I get another trial run?" Jiya asks.

"I don't know about all of that… I'll have to let you know, but I'll have to call you back."

"OK. Shavon says 'Hi' to you and Dayshanae. Talk to you later," she responds hanging up.

"Hey, Shavon says HI."

"Oh aiight, 'cause I was about to ask who you were disrespecting me with," Dayshanae says with a big smile on her face.

"Girl, you crazy," he says sitting beside her with a plate at the kitchen table.

"How am I crazy? Let a nigga call here you would wild the fuck out. And you know it…wouldn't you?"

"I on' know, I might," he says smiling.

"What you mean you don't know? You know you would."

"Like I said, I don't know…" he continues to repeat, being difficult.

"Boy, whateva, where's my plate at?"

"In the refrigerator."

"So you made your plate and forgot all about me?" Dayshanae says gaining an attitude.

"I didn't forget you, it's wrapped up in the refrigerator."

"Whateva, let your punk-ass put cut yourself," Dayshanae says storming out of the kitchen.

Being used to Dayshanae's babyish walk-out scenes, Kashmere finishes his plate and heads home.

At home he finds Sinsation sitting on his porch awaiting his arrival.

"So what's up with you?"

"Where you been stranger?" she asks him as he walks up on the porch.

"I've been chilling and what the fuck you doing at my house?" he questions his uninvited guest.

"I wanted to see you and ask why you weren't returning my calls."

"Man, fuck the calls, what about my damn car?" He screamed.

"You talking to me now, aren't you? It seems like I got your attention."

"You know what...." he begins to say deciding not to finish his statement.

"What? No, finish saying what you were about to say," Sinsation suggests grabbing onto his arm.

"First of all, get your fucking hands off of me!" he shouts removing her grip from him. "Second, I didn't say shit. So, I wasn't going to say shit."

"Boy, don't play with me. Please don't... I hate when people play with me."

"Is that a threat?"

"Trust me, it's no threat, but I assure you it's a promise," she says now standing in front of him face to face. "Look Kashmere, I really like you...I really do," she adds on in a seductive kind of way, rubbing her hand up his thigh as she spoke.

"So if you like me, why the fuck you act the way you act?" he questions removing her hand.

"I don't know. Look, just put it like this, I don't want you with anybody else. That friend of yours down there and your tongue are too precious to let go," she answers looking downward.

"Oh really."

"Really. If you going to be with Dayshanae, I have to respect that, but let me get that at least every week or two in a month if not every day or every other day."

"Damn, you straight to the point, huh?" Kashmere says as he begins to look around. "Look ain't shit going to happen, at least not out here," he continues to say winking his eye, leading her on.

"Then let's go inside then, nigga… Didn't I say stop playing with me?" Sinsation replies smiling in a sexy seductive way knowing she's got him where she wants him. Now comfortably inside, she sits on his plush leather couch as he goes upstairs.

While he's upstairs Kashmere takes off his sweatshirt leaving on only his sneakers, pants and white tank top known to all as a wife beater. It perfectly fit his muscular toned body.

Sinsation sneaks up the stairs to watch him change. While Sinsation looks on, thoughts of past experiences with him run through her mind. She remembers how Kashmere moved and felt inside of her. In her own pleasurable way, Sinsation half-closes her eyes, continuing to look on as her legs slowly open. Still not knowing he's not alone, Kashmere casually turns around.

"Oh shit, girl, you better announce yourself," Kashmere says not noticing the mood that she's in from her facial expressions. But he does notice that she's now dressed in nothing, only her Victoria Secret lace trim silk bra and thong, the things she is famously known to wear.

With her deep into her fantasy world, Kashmere looks on calmly. Sinsation takes matters in her own hands by removing her bra and gently caressing the points of her upper body that would catch the eye of any man.

Quietly looking on, Kashmere becomes fully erect, bulging through his sweats. Forgetting or not even caring that he is looking on she now reveals her garden of love, soaked unspeakably, dripping onto her fingers while at least three enter the soft walls of her inner temple. Making herself at home, Sinsation lays back enjoying her self-established fulfillment.

"Are you going to sit there and watch or are you going to give me that rooster as you peoples call it?" she moans out adding another finger to enhance the feeling.

"Don't mind me I'll look on for a couple of minutes then you'll like what I'll do next…"

"There you go playing with me again," she says, stopping everything and rushing his body like in a game of football. Pressing him against the wall she pulls down his sweats, slowly grazing the pole that she loves and yearns for.

Coat after coat, her taste buds demolish the now drenched lollipop she loves so much. Twirl after twirl her tongue travels up and down, and round and round tasting every drop. Now stiff and hard Sinsation turns around spreading her gates forcing him inside of her.

"Damn, girl…." Kashmere moans out as she works her ass clapping against his body. Gripping her ass at first, he realizes what he is doing and pulls her off.

"What are you doing?"

"Yo, this shit ain't right…"

"But it feels good, right?" she responds approaching him once again.

Tempting him more and more she begins to gently grip his friend, stroking it up and down. Trying his best to fight the temptation, the urge for more takes control leading the two to indulge into unexpected, wild, kinky pleasure causing Kashmere to become trapped in the bliss of wetness which rolls down his thighs in every motion.

Experiencing the same thing every time, full of satisfaction, Sinsation lays calm and silent, releasing her moisture. Leaving her alone, Kashmere goes to cleanse his body, angry at himself for what just took place.

"Shit what the fuck is wrong with me? When they said temptation is a MF they wasn't lying!" he thought out loud to himself as the warm water from the shower clings to his body.

While he's in the shower, Sinsation yells out goodbye and heads home smiling. Thinking to herself that she still has Kashmere to fool around with after everything.

Chapter twenty

Now having done Sinsation recently, Kashmere finds out that Jiya is now in DC waiting for him to come see her. With Dayshanae still acting childish and not calling, Kashmere calls her, leaving a message telling her he is going to DC. A few minutes after he leaves a message, Dayshanae is ringing his phone.

"So who are you going to see in DC and why is Sinsation calling my house telling me she was over your house?"

"First, I'm going to see a friend, why you worried about it? You wasn't calling me anyhow. I don't know why she is calling you. When I came home she was on my porch," Kashmere explains.

"So you screwing around with her again? Since I wasn't calling and she was around, you fuck her?!" Dayshanae explodes in fury.

"Who said I screwed her?"

"She did. You know what, I'm on my way!" she screams hanging up.

"Now I got to hear her mouth," he thinks aloud to himself.

Not really wanting to go through the drama, he waits for her to get all the bullshit out of the way. When Dayshanae arrives she starts to attack at the first sight of Kashmere's brown eyes.

"So now you messing with that Bitch? You know how I feel and you screw her?"

"Dayshanae. Dayshanae, you going to believe her over me…? That's the same broad that tried to kill both of us….remember?" Kashmere says rubbing her cheek gently looking into her eyes.

"But why would she call me? She never called me before and now all of a sudden she calls out of the blue, telling me all that shit."

Before she could finish, Kashmere kisses her trying to remove the thought from her head. Continuing to kiss her, Dayshanae forgets all about what they were fighting about and decides to kiss him back. Leaving Jiya waiting, Kashmere tends to more important business…keeping Dayshanae happy and drama free.

With his phone constantly ringing he ignores it as he starts to taste every bit of her delightful body.

"Answer your phone…" she moans out.

"So you want me to stop…?"

"Hell, no, I just wanted to act like I cared. You better not stop," she says grabbing his bald head, holding it in place right where she wants it.

"Don't front… Hey, if you want me to do this I got to breathe… Damn!"

"Oh, my bad, baby," she says loosening up on her grip.

Knowing he's in complete control he begins to take it to the next level. Keeping her pressed against the door she raises her leg and allows him to enter into her world.

Trying not to move, Dayshanae hops into his arms, wrapping her legs around Kashmere's waist. Catching her by gripping on the thing that is most noticed on her, they continue their voyage on satisfying each other.

Nails dig deep into inner layers of skin as their two bodies became aquainted once again.

Moving from the doorway to the couch, positions change. Still with legs wrapped around him and nails still engraved in skin, Kashmere tries to make new openings with her walls.

"Ummm....Ummmm shit..." she tries so hard to hold in.

Repeatedily she says the same phrase over and over again. Sucking upon her upper portion drives her more into the fantasy universe, wanting to try new things. Kashmere turns over as Dayshanae straddles him as usual. After two minutes they come face to face, but just for a moment.

Showing off her imagination, Dayshanae lays back and forms a human crab and tells Kashmere to do his damage. Not turning down the opportunity, he begins to work. Ten minutes of appreciating his talent, she lies on her back and requests Kashmere to take it easy and enjoy the satisfaction.

At least an hour later they're both knocked out asleep. When Kashmere wkes up, by the ringing of his phone, he can see that Dayshanae is gone. Being comfortable, stretched out across the couch, he unwantingly rolls over to answer it.

"Hello..." the sleepy voice of Kashmere answers.

"Wake up, boy," Dayshanae shouts, "I'm on my way back over there. We got to talk about something."

"Aiight, the door will be open. but I might be in the shower," he explained.

"Oh really...?"

"See look at you, your mind always in the gutter."

"You complaining?" she curiousily asks. "'Cause I can stop altogether, the talking, the sex, you know everything."

"Damn, I'm saying why you taking it to the extreme?" he responds laughing. Look girl, I'll see you when you get here."

"Aiight, bye."

"Bye."

Kashmere unlocks the door before he heads upstairs just like he promised, then he tries his best to be dressed by the time Dayshanae gets there. After he finally finishes, he comes downstairs. Dayshanae is stretched out just hanging up the phone with Mika.

"I swear, I wish that day with me, you and Mika never happened."

"Why! Whats wrong?" he asks pulling his t-shirt over his head.

"'Cause every time I talk to her she is always asking where you at. She slipped up a couple of days ago and today she said she wanted to screw you again."

"Damn, for real? And you thought I would be the one always asking about it," he said laughing.

"I know, but every time I talk with her your name always is coming up. I just gave in a minute ago and said it could happen tomorrow if you weren't busy. I said I had to talk to you first, though."

"So that's what you woke me up for?"

"Oh, naw, but since I told her that I'll wait until after tomorrow 'cause what I got to say might mess up the whole thing," she says with a little smile on her face. But I'm about to go back home and call her…and don't worry it's nothing bad."

"Oh, aiight 'cause I was ready to ask you. So your punk ass woke me up for nothing. Get out, punk!" Kashmere yells pushing her halfway out the door. "And don't call 'cause I'm going back to sleep… I tell you, black people these days!"

They both start laughing.

"Then leave us black people alone then…" she says laughing, walking out the door. "Take your lazy ass back to sleep."

"Oh yeah, I start this job working for Pepsi in the marketing department."

"That's good…but take your ass to sleep. Trust me, you'll need it for tomorrow," she says talking shit.

"Girl, whateva, bye."

The minute she was out of sight he also became out of sight under his covers fast asleep. When he was getting ready to go into his deep sleep, the phone rang once again.

"Hello?"

"Hello, can I please speak to Mr. Johnson?"

"This is he? Who's calling?"

"This is Shante Williams from the Pespi Company calling to confirm your training day starts Monday at 8 am."

"Oh, OK, I'll be there."

"OK, see you then."

Instead of just hanging up, Kashmere turns the ringer off so he can sleep undisturbed. Hours later he wakes up and sees that Jiya is the only person that called.

"Yo, Jiya what's up? Sorry I couldn't see you, something came up," he says when she picks up.

"You couldn't call?"

"Yo, I was with my shorty."

"Oh, aiight, well look I'll be back in DC in two weeks for this show, I hope I can see you then?" she suggests.

"We'll see…but I'm going to try to get some more sleep."

"Aiight, call me when you wake up, it doesn't matter the time."

"Aiight, I'll do that, but I'm not making no promises…"

"Oh, I know not to hold my breath, bye," Jiya says laughing.

"Aiight."

Kashmere tried hard as hell to fall back to sleep but he had no luck, so he called Dayshanae.

"Hey, cutie…"

"You just waking up you lazy bastard?" she jokes.

"Yeah, why?"

"'Cause damn, I smell your breath through the phone…"

"Man, screw you…" he laughs.

"I mean damn, boy, take care of that."

"Whateva, I'm too tired to argue," he responds in a very sleepy voice.

"Oh yeah, Mika said she was going to call you later about tomorrow."

"Aiight."

At that moment his phone clicks.

"Hold on…" he told her.

"Hello?"

"Can I speak to Kashmere?" the unfamiliar voice asks.

"Who this?"

"Mika."

"Oh, what's going on? Hold on, Dayshanae is on the other line."

"Aiight, tell her I'm going to call her later."

"Aiight, hold on." Kashmere clicks back over to Dayshanae. "Hey," Kashmere says.

"Yeah…?"

"That's her and she said she'll call you later," he tells her.

"Oh aiight, go talk to her 'cause mommy wants me anyways."

"Aiight, call me back."

"OK," she says hanging up.

"I'm back, what's going on?"

"Nothing. So did Dayshanae tell you about tomorrow?" Mika asks.

"Yeah, and she told me how you were asking about me."

"I'm not going to lie. Yeah, I was. Shit, if you get something good you'll always want it again. Don't you agree?" Mika explains and asks all in the same statement.

"I hear that, and hell yeah, if I get something good. And if it's good enough, I'll never let it go."

"I'm not trying to let you go, but Dayshanae got a tight hold on your ass. So I got only our sharing session to have you," she says.

"Oh really, I hear you talking."

"But I'll be around there like 1:00 pm, if that's aiight?"

"Yeah, just call me," Kashmere says.

"Aiight, I hope that good shit wasn't only a one time thing."

"Trust me, it wasn't. I keep the quality good, if not better."

"We'll see…"

"We sure will," he responds as they both hang up.

Chapter twenty-one

Just like she said, Mika arrived at one o'clock exactly, catching Kashmere minutes after he stepped out of the shower. She knocked on the door for a couple of minutes until Kashmere finally opened the door, wrapped in a towel still with water running down his chest.

"Hey, what's up? Where's Dayshanae?" He asked looking around.

"Home I guess; I got to call her."

"Oh, aiight, well come on in…"

"Did I come at a bad time or a real good time?" Mika asked biting her bottom lip.

"You tell me…" he says turning to go upstairs.

Not answering him, she basically follows him upstairs. In the middle of the stairs, Mika pulls the entire towel from around Kashmere's body bearing his smooth skinned rump.

"Damn, can't you wait until your girl gets here?"

"I can call her. I mean, you can 'cause my mouth will be full."

"Your mouth will be full? How you figure?" he asks sitting on the side of the bed reaching for the phone. As he begins to dial, Mika answers his question.

"Yeah, it's going to full" she says sliding the key to women's entry deep into her mouth. The moment Dayshanae answers the phone all she can hear is Kashmere enjoying himself.

"Hello, what the hell are you doing?" she screams.

"Oh damn, my bad, your girl is here and she is not trying to wait for you…" Kashmere struggles to get out without a moan following behind it.

"I'm on my way," Dayshanae says hanging up.

"Is the door unlocked?" Kashmere asks Mika.

"Yeah," Mika responds going right back to what she was doing. Ten minutes later, Dayshanae walks in the room to find Kashmere laid back on the bed with Mika licking on his succulent log that she seems to love so much. Refusing to not be involved, she quickly undresses and climbs into the bed to find Kashmere ready to taste her garden of love.

"Hi, Dayshanae," Mika says in between each lick.

"Umm…my bad, at least I'm here now," Dayshanae moans her response.

Returning back to their exotic escapade, Dayshanae switches positions with Mika, giving Mika the chance to once again get tasted as she swallowd the mandingo structure inch by inch. Trying not to choke herself to death, Dayshanae gives his structure instant access by doing what she does best, bouncing her womanhood onto Kashmere.

Noticing that Dayshanae has hopped aboard, Mika turns to face her still positioned on Kashmere tasting post. Mika started to kiss upon Dayshanae lips and upper body. Releasing two overpowering orgasms, Mika focuses to feel Kashmere within Dayshanae's walls.

"Hold up I'm cumming right now," Dayshanae screamd out as Mika licks upon her tip which lies within the outer edges of Dayshanae's walls, causing her gentle release to become an unbearable explosion making Dayshanae the first female to scratch her back from her waistline to the bottom of her neck. Experiencing this for the first time, Mika screams.

"Ouch!"

"I'm sorry… I'm so sorry," Dayshanae cries out seeing what she's done. "Come on girl, get that pain off your mind."

With her back in pain, Mika bends over with her face disappearing in a pillow as she arches her back to fill the halls of her insides.

"Damn, boy, do you have to feel so damn good?" Mika asks. Hearing this statement, jealousy builds up inside of Dayshanae feeling that Mika is enjoying what's hers too much.

"Hurry up and cum, nigga," Dayshanae yells just before Mika throws Kashmere on his back.

Once on his back, Mika seems to go insane driving her nails deep into his waist.

"Get up, I'm about to cum," Kashmere yells out, feeling the condom bursting.

"Go ahead and cum, you got a condom on," Mika responds moving faster.

"Yo, get up…the shit bust," he tries to get out but can't hold back the inner substance pushing it's way out.

Thinking and hoping he pushed her off in time, they all watch the releasing of his power onto his stomach.

"Damn, that's a lot," Dayshanae says looking at him.

"What you were backed up or something?"

"I guess so…"

"Well anyway that's too much shit to be wasting" Mika yells out licking up every noticable drop.

"That's how you feel?" Kashmere questions looking on.

Watching her girl in action the anger rises up to a boiling point.

When Mika is long gone, Dayshanae explodes.

"You need to stop fucking her like that, she's enjoying you too much for me," she screams while Kashmere takes his shower. "I promise you that shit will never happen again!"

"That's what I thought before today, but it was your idea for today…so you need to stop fussing. Like I said, it was your idea," Kashmere says looking her up and down as she steps into the shower to join him.

"I know it was my idea… I apologize for yelling, but that shit pissed me off…her saying that you feel so damn good," she explains rubbing along his chest. "Oh yeah, remember I said I had to tell you something but I wanted to get this bullshit day out of the way?"

"Yeah, what's going on?" Kashmere asked standing under the flowing water.

"I'm pregnant, but I don't know how far I am."

Silent and still, Kashmere sits quietly scaring Dayshanae with his silence. "Kashmere…are you aiight."

"Yeah, I'm aiight…" he says smiling, he'd always wanted a seed of his own.

"What, you happy?"

"Hell, yeah…" he screamd hugging her. "You know how long I wanted a child?"

Kashmere was not reacting like the average man. Dayshanae hugs him back even though she is shocked as hell.

Following the shower they had a long open-hearted conversation expressing their feelings about the situation. After hours of talking they came to the conclusion that they should have the baby.

Weeks go by with no drama between Kashmere and Dayshanae, spending every day together. Everything is going good until Mika calls Dayshanae. Dayshanae is still upset at her reaction about being with Kashmere, so Dayshanae tries to hide her jealousy.

Finally, Dayshanae told Mika she's pregnant with Kashmere's baby. Expressing her happiness, Mika congratulates Dayshanae. They talk for at least an hour calmly, then argue for another hour. The moment they hang up the phone, Dayshanae speeds to Kashmere's.

She finds him in the middle of taking all these baby supplies out of his trunk.

"Kashmere…" she screams.

"What's up, ma, you OK?"

"Hell, naw, I think we need to go in the house."

Dropping everything back into the trunk thinking something's wrong with the baby, he grabs Dayshanae and races her to the couch.

"Is it the baby?"

"I just don't believe what the fuck I just heard."

"What?" Kashmere says curiously.

"Did Mika call you?"

"I saw her number on the phone, but I was in the store when she called, why?"

"She's pregnant!!!"

"What! Don't bullshit me!" he screams.

"Why the fuck would I bullshit about something like that? So, I guess you got two baby mothers now 'cause she got her mind made up that she's keeping it."

"Damn."

"Damn, my ass, I know we shouldn't have done that shit!" she says crying. Now my girl's pregnant, by my baby's father."

"I'm sorry, boo, neither one of us planned the pregnancies, but I have to take on the responsibility of both babies since you both are keeping them," he explained. "Oh yeah, I got the job at the Pepsi company," he adds.

"Like you really need the job," Dayshanae says.

"I just need something constructive to do with my time," Kashmere explaind.

"That's good, boy, but I need to go home and think this thing through. I'm not mad at you 'cause you were satisfying my wants, I'm mad at the situation. Call me later, OK," she says closing the door behind her.

Opening the door to catch her, he screams out her name as she ignores him pulling off to go home. Calling Mika and talking to her for hours about the baby, he explains he would be there for his child. He also tells her that she needs to talk with Dayshanae because they're friends and they need to decide what was going to happen between them. Not hanging up, Mika calls Dayshanae so they all can talk about the subject.

"Hello?" Dayshanae answers.

"Hey, girl, I know you are upset but I think you, me and Kashmere should talk. He's on the phone right now," Mika explains.

"Look I know Kashmere will be there for the both of us and I'm not mad, 'cause I know him. I'm just upset at the situation with us both being pregnant at the same time. I just have to get adjusted to the idea of both of us being pregnant," Dayshanae tries to explain without crying.

"Hey, Dayshanae, I understand what you're saying but I feel I need to still apologize," Kashmere says.

"Me, too, you know I'm never trying to hurt you 'cause you my girl," Mika says. "You know me and Kashmere love you."

"I love ya'll, too… I just got to get used to both of us being pregnant. Look, I'm tired as shit so Kashmere, go see Mika 'cause I know you want to make sure she is aiight, carrying your baby in all. After that, come over in a couple of hours to wake me up," Dayshanae says minutes before she hangs up.

"Hey, Mika, give me your address and I'll be on my way."

Gathering all her information, he heads over to her house. When he arrives Mika answered the door wrapped in a robe wearing nothing underneath.

"Hey, what's up?"

"Nothing, waiting for you to come over," she answers loosening her robe.

"Waiting for me to do what?"

"Just come in," she says pulling him in the door.

Pressed against the door, Mika kneels down to give pleasure to her baby's father.

"Yo, you need to stop," he moans out pushing her head away.

"Why? Dayshanae can't get mad. You my baby's father, too, she should also know I'm going to be in need."

"I feel what you saying, but naw I can't do it right now. Look, I'll be back. Let me go get some baby stuff," he says leaving for the store.

"Make sure you come back."

"I will!" Kashmere yells as he pulls off.

With them both being pregnant, Kashmere starts to understand the drama that is about to occur during and after the pregnancies.

Ka'Shus

Chapter twenty-two

Trying to equally spend time with Dayshanae and Mika, Kashmere sits home stressed. Having Dayshanae as a baby mother is cool, she doesn't ask for anything, or argue about anything. All she wants is quality time like always. Now Mika, on the other hand, is asking for everything already, everything on TV. She argues if Kashmere is on the same side of the street with another girl and truly can't understand that Kashmere has to spend time with her along with Dayshanae. While at home, Mika calls Kashmere to do her check ups.

"Kashmere, what are you doing?" She questions.

"Nothing, about to walk out the door to go to the doctor's with Dayshanae."

"Why can't she go by her damn self?"

"'Cause she's also carrying my baby and I'm going to every appointment just like I go to yours," Kashmere says with a little attitude. "Since you're asking questions about why she can't go by herself, why can't you go by your damn self?"

"'Cause my baby's father told me he was going with me!" she screamed.

"OK, and like you I told her I'd go with her to all her appointments at least a day before or a day after all your appointments. Also, all these appointments are interfering with my new job. They are getting sick of me taking time off. But look, I got to pick her up so I'll call you when I get back."

"Whateva, boy," she says slamming down the phone.

Already used to Mika's ignorant attitude, he pushes the way she hung up out of his mind and heads to go pick up Dayshanae so they won't be late. When he arrives, Dayshanae is waiting for him sitting on her porch talking to her mom.

"Took you long enough, you punk," Dayshanae says laughing.

"Whateva girl, come," he says as he walks up on the porch kissing Ms. Brenda. "Well, if you leave my mother alone we can go."

"You just lucky you carrying my baby 'cause if you weren't I might be forced to thrash…." He says laughing.

"Whateva, boy…" she says laughing, walking towards the car.

"See what I go through, ma…see what your daughter puts me through?" he says turning to Ms. Brenda while walking off the porch.

"Hey, that's between you and her. Don't put me in it," she responds laughing as she walks into the house.

In the car, Dayshanae sits there listening to "RL" of Next's new CD. "You keep getting smart aiight…I'm going to push the baby back up in you for another nine months," Kashmere says laughing.

"Hell, no you ain't."

"Anyways, how you doing? You aiight?"

"Yeah, I'm OK…and if I wasn't, you would know," she explains.

"Let me tell you all the drama I went through with your girl today."

"I already know… She left me like three messages talking about how I'm taking all your time from her."

"Yo, she crazy for real…. Damn, I thought I was spoiled. She tops every spoiled person out there," he says.

"Yeah, she spoiled, she's used to her men spoiling her," Dayshanae tells him.

"But I'm not her man and I am gonna tell her."

"I know, you're worse. A man can leave her with no drama. You can leave but have a lifetime of drama, since you're her baby's daddy."

"See what listening to you got me?" he says as Dayshanae starts to laugh. "It ain't funny."

"I know 'cause I go through drama, too, but I'm laughing at you 'cause you look so cute when you're mad!" she says rubbing on his cheek.

"Whateva, don't touch me."

"Ahhh, poor baby."

After hassling their way through traffic, they finally reached Mercy Hospital on Calvert in downtown Baltimore. Luckily, they were able to make their appointment. Dayshanae's OB/GYN checks on the baby, then sits down and talks to them, assuring them the baby is fine. Hearing this brightens up their day until they reach the car and his phone rings, showing Mika's number on the caller ID.

"Here go your girl…" he says.

"Gimme that damn phone," she says answering it but not saying anything.

"I know you finished with her by now…and you need to bring your ass over here. She had enough of your time, I need some!" Mika shouts, not knowing Kashmere's not on the phone.

"Excuse me, this is Dayshanae and no he's not finished with me, 'cause just like you I need some, too," she says laughing. She hands him the phone. "It's your other babymother."

As he sighs and takes the phone he waits to hear her mouth.

"Hello?"

"So I guess I'm not seeing you today, huh?" She asks with an attitude.

"Look, I'll be over there later."

"Whateva, bring your ass over here now!" she explodes hanging up the phone.

"Your girl going to make me hurt her, for real."

"Calm down, boo, I'll make you feel better when we get back to my house," Dayshanae says rubbing his thigh.

"We'll see…." he says smirking.

At Dayshanae's they find that Ms. Brenda's gone and the stove is still filled with pots and pans with food. Letting Dayshanae change her clothes, Kashmere fixes her a plate and sits it on the table. Not really hungry, he just grabs a little plate.

When Dayshanae sees his plate she quickly questions him. "Is that all you're eating?"

"Yeah, I'm not really hungry."

"You OK, boo, 'cause your greedy ass always got at least two plates already made," she says laughing.

Kashmere sits back, not saying a word, then instantly gets up, making Dayshanae even more worried. Grabbing his arm before he passes her, Dayshanae shows that she's really concerned.

"Kashmere, what's wrong?"

"Nothing. I'm going to the bathroom," he says.

"OK, you can be going to the bathroom, but something is bothering you."

"I'm aiight, for real."

"Aiight, you know I'm here for you, boo."

"I know…you always been," he replies smiling.

Letting him go and continuing to eat, Dayshanae sits quiet knowing something's on his mind. So when he returns she asks him again.

"What's wrong and don't lie…" Dayshanae demands.

"I'm just stressed…not with you, but with Mika always on my back bitching about everything."

"Boo, don't let her get to you… See, she knows you'll always be there since that's your baby…" she says. "Just stop thinking about her for right now OK, for me?"

"Aiight."

They continue to talk until Dayshanae finishes her plate.

To relax, Dayshanae forces him upstairs. He lies across her bed rubbing her stomach. Feeling stress-free now, he falls asleep along with Dayshanae wrapped in his arms. Not even an hour goes by and Mika is calling again.

"Hello?" he answers in a dry sleepy voice.

"What the hell are you doing?" she screams.

"Yo, I'm sleep."

"Where's Dayshanae?"

"Right here… I'm sleep."

"Get your ass up and come over here. She can sleep by her damn self," Mika screams loud enough that Dayshanae wakes up.

"Gimme the phone," Dayshanae says taking the phone.

"Hey, Mika, stop tripping and let him get some damn sleep. If he not running behind me, he behind you… I know he's both of our babies' father, but we got to at least give him some time to his self."

"OK, I feel what you saying but why he got to get his free time laying beside you?" Mika asks her firmly.

"For one, I'll let him go home and for two, I don't stress him like you do."

"Whateva, damn I wish I wasn't pregnant by the same nigga as you."

"Well, I know I don't believe in it, but I don't know how you feel, but ain't nobody forcing you to keep the baby," Dayshanae said.

"I know…maybe I won't keep the baby, I was already thinking about getting an abortion…but tell Kashmere trust me, he don't have to go with me tomorrow. I'll find somebody else who can be here 24/7 and will go whether it's a man or a female!" Mika screams hanging up the phone again.

Also ignoring her attitude, Dayshanae turns to a worn out sleepy Kashmere. Deciding not to bother him she allows him to sleep peacefully.

Chapter twenty-three

A few months pass and the drama calms down a little. Still carrying the same petty attitude, Mika only calls Kashmere to let him know what's going on with the baby. The last time he speaks with her the baby isn't doing very well. Being scared to death, Kashmere like always explains the situation to Dayshanae and she tells him he should be with Mika during Mika's hard times. If she needs him she will call. So from that day he starts spending more time with Mika.

Kashmere feels Mika's stomach.

"That feels good," Mika says rubbing Kashmere's head.

"OK, how the baby feeling? Are you still having those pains?"

"No, can you go get me a cup of water?"

"Yeah, that's all you want?" he asks making sure to grab everything all at one time.

"That's it. I ate before you came over."

"Oh, aiight."

Downstairs, he rinses out a glass. As he opens the refrigerator, he quickly catches an attitude. The reason for the attitude is because when he glances through the refrigerator, there on the top shelf is a half bottle of Hennessy. "What the hell?" he says to himself.

Forgetting the water, Kashmere grabs the bottle and runs upstairs.

"Whose bottle is this?" he angrily asks.

"Not mine, it's my little cousin's" she responds.

"Is your cousin a boy or a girl and when did they leave it?"

"It's a boy, and it's been at least a week," she responds. "Why are you questioning me?"

"'Cause you are a lying ass bitch!" he explodes.

"How you figure?"

"'Cause first of all, there's a glass right there on your nightstand with the same color lipstick you got on now and it got some fresh ice floating in it."

"OK I had a couple of drinks…so what?" she responds as she picks up the glass right in front of him.

"That's why your damn stomach hurts…"

"The baby will be aiight! Shit, stop trippin', you."

Before she can finish her statement, she receives a very sharp pain in her stomach as blood rushes down her leg and she's bent over.

"Kashmere! Kashmere!"

"What?" he screams, not noticing all the blood.

"I think I'm having a miscarriage," Mika responds as her body becomes an instant puddle of blood. Clot after clot falls as the pain surges through her body.

"What should I do?" Kashmere asks full of shock and not able to think.

Thinking it was all over, she simply asks for something to clean the mess up. The moment Kashmere goes out of the room the pain erupts again.

"Kashmere! Kashmere!" Mika screams as the lifeless baby exits itself onto the bed.

"What…what?" He runs in seeing what's just happened.

As he slowly walks to the bed, Kashmere sees his baby dead. He grabs a pillowcase and wraps it up with tears running down his face. Mika is lying there in shock. "Hurry, come on so we can go to the hospital!"

"OK."

She needed him to assist her 'cause she couldn't move.

Hours later, Kashmere's in the waiting room while Mika's in emergency. While he waits, Kashmere calls Dayshanae and tells her what has happened.

"Where are ya'll now?" She asks.

"We at University."

"I'm on my way," she says hanging up. Ten minutes later, Dayshanae walks in and stands over Kashmere hunched over. She sits next to him and holds him close.

"Are you OK?"

All Kashmere can say is there was blood everywhere and how he wrapped up the baby and brought it, too.

"I saw my baby die in front of my own eyes," Kashmere was still in shock.

"It's OK; let it out, boo. How is Mika? Have the doctors come out yet."

Dayshanae continued to hold him. Kashmere started to cry his heart out. Thirty minutes later the doctors inform them that Mika will have to stay a few nights for observation and testing. With them both allowed to stay with Mika, they sit on each side of her bed. After all the medication has worn off, Mika wakes up and notices that Dayshanae and Kashmere both are there by her side.

"Hey," Mika mumbles.

"What's up, shorty?" Kashmere asks.

"Did the baby die, where's the baby?" Mika cries.

"The baby didn't live Mika?"

Dayshanae asks Mika how she's feeling. "I'm aiight I guess. I apologize for how I have been acting the past couple of monthes."

"Girl, stop worrying, just worry about getting well," Dayshanae suggests to Mika. "I accept your apology 'cause you were tripping."

"Tripping ain't the word, she crazy," Kashmere says as all begin to laugh.

A week flies by and the three's friendship is good as ever. Mika found a new girlfriend and was not really coming around. That gave Kashmere and Dayshanae more time to spend together.

Feeding Dayshanae and making sure she's OK, Kashmere heads home to get a few things. Finally, back at home after a couple days he calls back all the missed call numbers and grabs a few things he would probably need. Before he walks out the door to head back to Dayshanae's the phone begins to ring.

"Hello?"

"Hey, baby…" the soft voice says.

"Who is this?"

"Sinsation, what you don't know my voice now?" She says, "I bet you know it when you in my shit."

"Man, screw you….you young ass shot."

"What are you talking about?" she responds not knowing that he knows she called Dayshanae.

"So what…it's not like ya'll married or she your babymother or something," Sinsation says, unaware of the past months.

"We not married but she is carrying my baby."

Sinsation falls over the phone followed by a hang up. Proceeding to where he is going, Kashmere's cell starts to ring the minute he pulls up to Dayshanae's. Noticing that it's Sinsation, he answers knowing that she'll continue to call until he picks up.

"Yeah?" he answers.

"So that bitch's carrying your baby?"

"Whoa…don't disrespect her now, 'cause you phoney as shit. First you talk about her, then the minute something goes down you're running to her like she's your best friend or mother." he says calmly. "So to set everything straight, so it won't be no other drama don't call my house, my cell, or visit my damn house and don't even try to come to Dayshanae's either!" Kashmere adds screaming.

"Kashmere, why you acting like that…?"

"You heard me, right?"

"What?" she says.

"Did you hear what I said?" he asks again.

"Yeah, I heard you…"

"Good," he says hanging up and finally walking up to the porch.

Feeling that he has set Sinsation straight, he goes to find out what Dayshanae's doing.

"Hey babymama," he greets Dayshanae.

"Boy, don't call me that," Dayshanae responds laughing. "Guess who called today?"

"Who?"

"Just put it like this, didn't you tell somebody I was pregnant and to stop calling you?" she says smiling.

Kashmere starts laughing. "Damn, I couldn't even get in the damn house," he mutters to himself.

"Now I know who you talking about."

"You know she mad as shit, right… I guess you were suppose to be only her's," Dayshanae says still smiling.

"You better go 'head with that bullshit."

"Whatever, you need to stop fucking this broad out here."

"I ain't fucking nobody, just you and a couple of other people," Kashmere responds laughing.

"Keep playing with me here, and I will fuck you up, pregnant and all…" she says laughing, slapping his arms.

"You and what army…?"

"Keep trying me, aiight…"

"Whatever…so how's my baby doing?"

"I'm aiight…" she replies being cut-off instantly.

"Not you…my little baby right here…" Kashmere says rubbing her stomach.

"Forget you…"

As they begin to play fight then lie back and relax, they conversate over baby names.

"You like Tameka if it's a girl?" Dayshanae asks.

"Naw that's a freak name…"

"What? I got a friend and a cousin named Tameka."

"And they both are probably freaks…" he says laughing.

"Whatever, what kind of name is Kashmere?"

"Fuck you…" he says pulling her back to his chest.

"We'll think of something…"

"I hope so, but I don't know about you."

"What you mean?"

"Oh nothing, I know the name is going to be cool, but if he or she comes out acting like you I'm going to need Jesus here with me in person," she says laughing.

"Whatever, you'll love them just like you love, me."

"I know…'cause you my baby," Dayshanae says turning around hugging him.

Chapter twenty-four

Dayshanae just became seven months, and she was as big as a house. She refused to know from the doctor as to what the sex of the baby was. Kashmere and Dayshanae left the doctor's office just knowing that the baby was healthy.

"Why can't we know?" Kashmere asks.

"We will when I turn eight months, I just want to wait until then."

"Oh, but what's the difference, we going to know anyway," he says opening the car door for her. "I need to know so I can go buy my little one a wardrobe."

"Oh, Lord," she sighs.

"What?"

"I see you going to spoil the baby already."

"And your point?" he screams with excitement. "That's my baby," he adds smiling, rubbing on her stomach.

"Boy, you crazy."

"Tell me something I don't know."

They both laugh and when they reach Dayshanae's house, Ms. Brenda is out on the porch enjoying the sunlight and peeling potatoes. Having at least two pots already filled with peeled potatoes, she is working on filling the third and final pot.

"Hey, Ms. Brenda, you sure you got enough potatoes for the cookout?" Kashmere asks helping Dayshanae up the stairs.

"Yeah, two pots are for the potato salad and this one is for the mashed potatoes."

"Oh, aiight."

"Kashmere, can you get me some water? Please?" Dayshanae asks sitting beside her mother.

"Yeah, you something too, Ms. Brenda?"

"No, I'm OK baby…" she responds smiling.

Returning with a pitcher of water, Kashmere pours Dayshanae a glass, knowing they would be out there for a while.

"What else you need?" he asks.

"Nothing, I just need you to go get a bushel of crabs."

"OK, that's no problem…just let me know when…" he responds.

"Oh yeah, that girl Sinsation came by when ya'll was gone."

Looking all confused because they haven't heard or seen her in months, Dayshanae asks her mom what she wanted.

"What she say?"

"Nothing, she just said she was checking up on you and the baby."

"For real…" Dayshanae says.

"What's wrong with her checking up on you?" Ms. Brenda asks not being totally aware of all the drama. For the next hour Dayshanae and Kashmere explain the levels of craziness and the amount of drama Sinsation has caused.

"That girl is crazy and, Kashmere, you need to leave her alone," Ms. Brenda demands.

"I am, I told her to stop calling me and Dayshanae, and I told her not to come over here," he explains.

"I really don't trust her around Dayshanae."

"I don't think she'll do anything to the baby."

"Well I hope not, 'cause I did tell her about the cookout," Ms. Brenda says.

"Oh Lord," Kashmere sighs.

Ten minutes later, the family members begin to arrive, filling the front and backyard while Ms. Brenda is with two of her sisters, taking over the kitchen. While they sit on the porch with Dayshanae's favorite cousin, Sabrina, Ms. Brenda yells out to Kashmere to go get the crabs.

"I'll be back, boo," he says to Dayshanae as he walks towards the car.

"Hurry up, boy…"

"Aiight…"

On his way to get the crabs, Kashmere receives a call from Shavon. "Hey boy, how's Dayshanae and the baby?"

"You know they aiight," he responds smiling. "What's up with you?"

"Nothing, just laying across my bed at my mom's house."

"Oh, I heard your girl Jiya was mad at me. Or did she get over it?"

"She's over it, but she still got it set in her mind that she's going to screw you again," Shavon says laughing.

"She's crazy," he laughs walking into the crab house.

Continuing to talk to Shavon while he waits for the crabs, his phone beeps. Noticing that it is Dayshanae, he hangs up with Shavon and quickly answered the call.

"I'm still waiting for the crabs."

"Yo, fuck the crabs. That bitch, Sinsation, came up in here with three girls and banged the shit out of Dayshanae while she was in her room. We on our way to Mercy now," Dayshanae's cousin Ricky screams.

"Shit… I'm on my way…" Kashmere responds running to the car and speeding to the hospital.

When he arrives he is informed from Ms. Brenda that Dayshanae and the baby were alright.

"She's just banged up a little bit, but she's alright," she says still crying.

"Oh, aiight, I was so worried."

The minute he says that, the doctor comes out to give his remarks from the examination.

"Ms., your daughter, along with your granddaughter are perfectly OK."

"Granddaughter? I'm going to have a granddaughter?" Ms. Brenda said full of excitement.

"Is there something wrong?" the doctor asked.

"Oh no, Dayshanae just wanted to wait to find out what she was having until she was eight months," Ms. Brenda explains, looking back at Kashmere who was smiling.

"Oh, I apologize..."

"It's no problem, I wanted to know anyways," Kashmere says. "So I'm having a daughter..."

"Sorry about that. So you're Mr. Kashmere. Your girlfriend and daughter are alright."

Before the doctor could finish his statement a nurse called for him as she dashed out the ER.

"Doctor....doctor...the baby moved and is tangled up in the umbilical cord and we're losing pressure!"

"Oh God!" the doctor said running into ER. When he reached the ER they were yelling, "We are losing her, the pressure is still dropping."

The family sat frozen by the nurse's statement and the tears began to fall. After an hour of waiting, the doctor returned with his head hung low. "Mr. Kashmere I'm sorry... I'm so sorry; I tried everything I could... But we couldn't save your little girl."

Forgetting who was talking to him Kashmere snapped and attacked the doctor.

"You said she was alright. You said she was aiight...you said she was fucking aiight!" Kashmere screamed while Ms. Brenda along with three other family members grabbed hold of him.

Calm down, Kashmere, you got to calm down,". Ms. Brenda consoled him as he cried his heart out.

When everything was calm and Kashmere was comforting Dayshanae, the doctor entered the room where Dayshanae was and explained what happened.

"Usually what we do when an unborn child is lost, we allow the parents to name the baby and they both receive a birth and death certificate…but it's your decision."

"Boo, you can name her 'cause I know how much you wanted a daughter," Dayshanae says to Kashmere.

"You sure?"

"Yeah, baby, just make it cute, please?" she responds smiling.

"I will…just give me a minute," Kashmere becomes silent then he says "Do you like Taliya Ra'e Johnson?"

"I like Taliya, but Ra'e?" she asks.

After Kashmere writes the spelling of the name, Dayshanae quickly falls in love with it. "That's so cute, a little ghetto, but it's cute."

"Whatever, girl, do you want to keep it or what?" he says.

"It's cool."

"Aiight," Kashmere says handing the written name to the doctor.

"OK, give me a few minutes and I'll have everything for the both of you…" the doctor says. "You won't have the certificates today, but you will receive the papers to take to vital records. In a couple of days take them to city hall and the certificates will be ready," he added.

"Oh, OK…thanks, doctor," Kashmere says shaking his head.

Chapter twenty-five

Tattoed with the name of his lost daughter, Kashmere lays beside Dayshanae as she admires his new artwork. "It's cute."

"Thanks, I just wish it didn't have 'rest in peace' above it," he responds hanging his head low.

"Boo, it's OK, it wasn't our time," she consoles him.

"Oh, did you hear Sinsation got her ass whipped?"

"For real, by who?"

"My cousins, when they found out I lost Taliya they went to look for her…and they found her at a bar with her friends bragging about what she did. They whipped their asses on the spot," she says.

"Damn," Kashmere says laughing. "My bad…my bad, it ain't funny. Naw, fuck that it's funny as hell," he continues to laugh.

"You're ignorant," she says laughing.

"I'm ignorant, but you laughing, too…whatever."

They both continued to laugh for a good five minutes when Kashmere's phone began to ring. With the phone next to her, Dayshanae answered it.

"Hey, girl," she says seeing Shavon's name on the caller ID.

"Hey, Dayshanae, how's the baby doing?" Shavon asks not having spoken to Kashmere since the crab store.

Before she begins to explain what happened, Dayshanae tells Kashmere who it is and asks him to grab them something to eat from the kitchen.

While he's gone, Dayshanae returns to telling Shavon the situation. Returning with two full plates of food Kashmere begins to eat while Dayshanae picks at her food, still on the phone.

"How about this, tell Shavon to call your house so a nigga like me can have his cell," he says. "I mean, damn, I know it's free but can I talk on my own phone?"

"Girl, call me on my phone, the big baby is crying for his phone," Dayshanae says giving Shavon the number and hanging up. When Shavon calls on her phone, Dayshanae hands Kashmere his cell phone.

"Here's your phone, you big baby."

"Whatever," he says taking the phone and placing it beside him.

"I thought you wanted to use it."

"No, I just felt left out 'cause ya'll wasn't talking to me and I had to say something," Kashmere replies laughing.

"You know what? Forget you. You too damn ignorant."

"Thank you," he says returning to his meal.

Continuing her conversation with Shavon, Dayshanae lies back and starts to eat her food.

When he finishes his food, Kashmere grabs the phone so that Dayshanae can finish eating.

"What's country?"

"Nothing, boy, sorry to hear about the baby."

"I'm trying to survive; I'm going to visit Rodney in a few," Kashmere tells Shavon.

"You know your girl's still asking about you."

"For what?"

"I told you she wants to screw you again," Shavon replies laughing.

"Well, the shit ain't going to happen."

"I know and I told her, but she's in denial."

"Hey, that's her problem," Kashmere says being his ignorant self.

While Shavon talked in one ear, Dayshanae tapped Kashmere and started whispering to him.

"I need to talk to you when I come back."

"Where you going?"

"Nowhere," Shavon says.

"Not you...Dayshanae," Kashmere says.

"To the bathroom..." Dayshanae says walking out the door.

"Oh," he replies to Dayshanae.

"Hey, Shavon."

"What's up?" she answers.

"I'm going to talk with you later."

"Aiight...bye and be safe, boy," Shavon says as they both hang up.

Just before Dayshanae returns Kashmere runs downstairs, placing the empty plates in the sink.

"Sit down, Kashmere, I need to talk to you about something," Ms. Brenda says. She was sitting at the kitchen table watching TV.

"What's going on, ma?"

"Look, the moment my daughter laid eyes on you she couldn't stop talking about you. Even my mother, as you know, always said ya'll would end up together. And like my daughter and mother, you know I love you very much no matter what happens between you two," she says smiling.

"I love you, too, ma...and you know I love your daughter with all my heart. Your family has been by my side since middle school... I'm not planning on trying to go anywhere."

"That's good to hear, now come give me a hug, boy," Ms. Brenda responds hugging him as she begins to cry.

"You OK?"

"Yeah, baby, I'm just happy Dayshanae has finally found someone that really loves her," she says continuing to hold him tight. When they finish hugging, Kashmere returns upstairs to find Dayshanae sitting silent in her room.

"So what's going?" he says sitting on her bed.

"Well this is really hard for me to talk about 'cause I'm really not the type of person to just come out and express my feelings…but as long as you've known me you should know that, right?"

"Oh, I know, but don't force yourself. Just tell me when you're ready…" Kashmere suggests.

"Naw, I'm ready to tell you now. It's just kinda hard with what I have to say. The shit is unexpected."

"Oh really, what?"

"Look, every since we met I had a crush on you but I never expressed my feelings until we got older and since we've been together, not thinking about all the drama, I enjoyed every bit of my time with you," she says beginning to cry. "It hurt me dearly when we lost Taliya 'cause I know you loved her with all your heart and also knowing that you would have been the best father to her."

"Here," he says handing her a box of tissues.

"Thanks, but like I was saying or trying to say is: I love you and I promised my grandmother I wouldn't never let you go, 'cause since the first day I said your name and then introduced you to my family she always said we would be together. We always laughed, thinking she was crazy."

"We sure did," he responds.

"But I never saw what she saw in you until I was pregnant with your child and you were there even though Mika was also carrying your child. I wish my grandmother was here right now, but I know she's smiling down on us since we made it through all the drama," Dayshanae says as she goes into her drawer.

"Look I'm going to stop beating around the bush. The reason I'm telling you all this is 'cause I wanted you all to myself forever and I'm never trying to lose you," she explains as she dropped to her knee. "I'm not used to this bullshit."

As she drops down, Kashmere freezes full of shock at what is going down.

"Kashmere, I love you and will you marry me?"

Silence fell over the both of them as Kashmere started to feel like he was the female of the relationship.

"Yea, shorty, you know I will," he responds as she slides the ring on his finger and starts to kiss him.

They both give the good news to Ms. Brenda and they all rejoice for a good hour. After all the tears are shed, Kashmere leaves to visit Rodney. When he arrives he does his usual, laying flowers across the grave and kneels down to talk.

"What's up…I know you already know what just happened, but if you don't 'cause your up there 'macking, well, me and Dayshanae are getting married. Don't say nothing 'cause I know you and her grandmother told us this was going to happen. But that's not all I wanted to tell you. I made you a promise that you'd be my best man…well I'm keeping my promise, your name will be in the program and I'll drop one off for you."

Kashmere began to cry. "Yo cuzin, I miss you and I love you," he says wiping his eyes.

Kashmere looks down at the gravesite and then into the heavens.

"I love you, cuzin…" he whispers as he slowly walks away into the setting sun.

His name is Ka'Shus pronounced "cautious." He was born in Baltimore, MD. Coming from a creative family he allowed his imagination to come to life through his writing. As an inspired Model and Actor, Ka'Shus has the mind set to satisfy the wants and needs of his audience. Now teamed with Kendall Publication he's able to release his first novel "Unexpected Love."

You can reach Ka'Shus at: www.myspace.com/kashus1ne

9 780979 187636

CPSIA information can be obtained
at www.ICGtesting.com
Printed in the USA
LVOW03s0110240418
574641LV00001B/113/P